For more than forty years,
Yearling has been the leading name
in classic and award-winning literature
for young readers.

Yearling books feature children's
favorite authors and characters,
providing dynamic stories of adventure,
humor, history, mystery, and fantasy.

Trust Yearling paperbacks to entertain,
inspire, and promote the love of reading
in all children.

OTHER YEARLING BOOKS YOU WILL ENJOY

TOAD RAGE, *Morris Gleitzman*

DON'T PAT THE WOMBAT!, *Elizabeth Honey*

HOW TO EAT FRIED WORMS, *Thomas Rockwell*

CRASH, *Jerry Spinelli*

DONUTHEAD, *Sue Stauffacher*

SPACE RACE, *Sylvia Waugh*

HOW ANGEL PETERSON GOT HIS NAME, *Gary Paulsen*

BILLY CLIKK: CREATCH BATTLER, *Mark Crilley*

UNDER THE WATSONS' PORCH, *Susan Shreve*

SKINNYBONES, *Barbara Park*

TOAD HEAVEN

MORRIS GLEITZMAN

A YEARLING BOOK

Text copyright © 2001 by Creative Input Pty Ltd.
Illustrations copyright © 2001 by Rod Clement

Visit us on the Web! www.randomhouse.com/kids

Educators and librarians, for a variety of teaching tools, visit us at
www.randomhouse.com/teachers

ISBN: 0-375-82765-X

Reprinted by arrangement with Random House Children's Books

Printed in the United States of America

January 2006

10 9 8 7 6 5 4 3 2 1

OPM

For Tom and Jamie

G'DAY FROM THE AUTHOR

You might notice a few strange and exotic words in this book. Fear not! They won't hurt you, they're just Australian. To find out what they mean, choose one of the following options.

1. Put the book down, fly to Australia, ask a local, fly back, pick up the book, resume reading.
2. Have a squiz at the glossary on page 191.

Happy reading,

Morris Gleitzman

Morris Gleitzman

Limpy stuck his head out of the grass and peered up and down the highway. He felt his crook leg twitching and his warts tingling like they always did when he was excited.

And scared.

All clear. No headlights speeding out of the darkness. No trucks, cars, buses, or caravans thundering along the highway. No humans on wheels looking for cane toads to squash.

"Let's do it," said Limpy.

"Do what?" said Goliath.

Limpy sighed. He told himself to stay calm. He told himself not to even think about whacking Goliath round the head with a lump of possum poo.

"Goliath," pleaded Limpy, "try to concentrate."

"I haven't had any dinner yet," grumbled Goliath. "I'm so hungry I could eat a human's hairbrush."

Limpy gripped his cousin's big arms.

"We've got a plan, remember?" said Limpy. "If it works, it'll improve the lives of cane toads everywhere."

"What?" sneered a nearby bull ant. "Even the ones that are already flat?"

Limpy ignored the bull ant.

In the glow from the railway-crossing light, he saw that Goliath was frowning.

"This plan," said Goliath. "I still don't get it."

"Do exactly what I told you," said Limpy, "and you will."

Goliath nodded uncertainly.

"It'll never work," sneered the bull ant. "You cane toads are losers."

Limpy didn't eat the bull ant. What he and Goliath were about to do was too important to waste time having a snack.

"Good luck, Goliath," said Limpy.

His cousin didn't reply. Limpy could see that a frown was still creasing Goliath's big warty face.

Poor thing, thought Limpy. Probably as tense as me. Or else he's got a stink beetle stuck in his throat.

Limpy turned to Uncle Nick, who was lying at the edge of the road.

"Good luck, Uncle Nick," said Limpy.

Uncle Nick didn't reply either. Limpy would have been surprised if he had. Uncle Nick had always been a silent sort of bloke, even before he was squashed flat by a truck and baked hard by the Queensland sun.

"Sorry about this next bit," added Limpy.

Limpy dipped a flat stick into the soft drink can he'd filled with sticky sap from the sticky sap tree. Gently he smeared sticky sap all over Uncle Nick. He knew Uncle Nick probably wouldn't be too happy about it if he was alive. From the expression on Uncle Nick's squashed face, he didn't look too happy about it now.

"I'll wash it off afterward," promised Limpy.

Struggling with the weight, Limpy picked Uncle Nick up, careful not to touch his sticky side, and handed him to Goliath.

"You sure you know what to do?" panted Limpy.

Goliath's frown had got bigger, like the time he'd tried to swallow a giant stick insect and then realized it was the tailpipe off a bus.

For a moment Limpy was worried that Uncle Nick was too heavy for Goliath. But it couldn't be that. Goliath was twice as big as Limpy, and four times as strong.

Then Limpy realized why Goliath's forehead was so crumpled.

He was thinking.

"I still don't get how this is gunna work," complained Goliath. "I hate to say it, but I reckon that bull ant's right."

The bull ant gave a chortle of triumph that only stopped when Goliath ate him.

"I'll explain it again," said Limpy patiently. "To stay healthy, we need flying insects in our diet, right? Because they're rich in vitamins and minerals."

"And wings," said Goliath.

"Right," said Limpy. "And the place to find flying insects is on the highway under the railway-crossing light. Which makes us easy targets for humans in vehicles. There's nothing a human in a vehicle likes better than driving over a cane toad, right?"

"That and picking their noses," said Goliath. "Lucky mongrels. Wish I had a couple of little cupboards in my face."

Limpy interrupted before Goliath forgot the plan again.

"Okay," said Limpy. "On the count of three. One, two, . . ." He checked that the highway was still clear and gave a signal to the family members waiting in the grass on the other side.

". . . three!"

Goliath grumbled some more, flexed his muscly arms, arched his back, and flung his round flat dry sticky uncle high into the air like a Frisbee.

It was a perfect throw.

"Well done," gasped Limpy.

High above them, Uncle Nick seemed to hover,

spinning in the cloud of insects flying around the railway-crossing light.

Limpy strained to see if any of them were getting stuck onto the sticky sap.

It looked like they were.

Then, suddenly, dazzling headlights roared round the bend in the highway. Huge wheels thundered over the railway tracks.

"A truck!" yelled Limpy.

He leaped into the ditch, dragging Goliath down after him, his hopes nosediving into the mud at the same time.

It's not fair, thought Limpy. No uncle should be hit by two trucks. Not on different nights. If this truck makes contact, Uncle Nick'll be smashed to bits. The family members on the other side could be injured by jagged pieces of flying uncle.

As the truck rumbled away into the night, Limpy peered anxiously up at the white haze over the railway crossing.

And saw, weak with relief, that Uncle Nick was still airborne. He was wobbling slightly but was still on course, spinning down toward the undergrowth on the other side of the highway.

Uncles and aunts, cousins and neighbors, were scrambling out of the ditch on the other side and hopping into position to catch Uncle Nick as he landed.

Some were so excited they jumped too soon and fell in a heap, which gave Uncle Nick something nice and soft to land on.

"It worked!" shouted the family members whose mouths weren't full of mud. "Good on you, Limpy and Goliath."

Limpy's warts tingled with delight.

He beckoned the family to bring Uncle Nick back through the stormwater tunnel under the road. As they emerged, Limpy looked anxiously to see how many flying insects Uncle Nick had stuck to him.

Not a huge number, but enough for a start.

Perhaps the sticky sap wasn't sticky enough, thought Limpy. I'll add a bit more mucus next time.

He turned to congratulate Goliath on a top throw. And saw that Goliath was still lying at the bottom of the ditch, face in the mud, sobbing.

"I knew it," Goliath was croaking, broad shoulders shuddering with misery. "I knew it was a dopey idea. I knew a truck would come. Now I've broken Uncle Nick."

Limpy tapped Goliath on the warts and pointed at the family faces grinning down at him.

Goliath blinked, sniffled, and stared up at Uncle Nick and his coating of insects.

"Stack me!" said Goliath, eyes widening. "Flying-insect pizza."

Limpy and the others chuckled. They'd never seen an actual pizza in real life because the pizza boxes humans threw out of cars only had bits of crust in them, but they knew what Goliath meant.

"Now I get it," said Goliath happily. "This is a way for us to collect flying insects without going onto the highway. And if we don't go onto the highway, humans can't run us over. Because humans only drive on the highway."

Limpy grinned. Goliath might be a bit slow, but he got there in the end.

The other cane toads applauded.

Goliath blushed modestly.

Then the happy group hurried toward the swamp to tell everyone else the good news and share the flying insects with them.

Limpy glowed with pleasure. Right up until a sudden violent noise made him spin round.

He froze in stunned disbelief, barely able to comprehend what he was seeing.

He'd never seen anything like it, not once in his whole life.

He heard Goliath and the others croak with amazed fear as they saw it too.

A vehicle, headlights blazing and motor revving, had driven off the highway and was crashing through the undergrowth, coming straight at them.

"Hide!" yelled Limpy.

He grabbed Goliath and dragged him into a bog hole.

The vehicle thundered toward them.

Limpy could feel Goliath's big warts trembling as they crouched in the mud.

I don't believe it, thought Limpy, trembling too. A vehicle driving through the bush. Away from the highway.

It wasn't natural.

"It isn't possible," croaked Goliath. "It can't be happening."

But it was.

Limpy gave Goliath's arm a reassuring squeeze, then peered out of the hole to make sure the others were safely hidden. They were. All around him in the moonlight Limpy could see legs and bottoms wriggling into hollow logs and clumps of weed. Out of the darkness came the sounds of other animals panicking.

"Look out!" croaked Goliath.

The vehicle roared past Limpy's face. It was so close Limpy felt his lips pulled out of shape by the slipstream and his mucus seared by diesel fumes.

He was still sneezing long after the vehicle had disappeared into the dark bush and its distant engine could be heard no more.

Limpy could still see it, though. The horrible image of its rear end bumping over rocks and logs was burned into his brain.

It was a four-wheel drive.

Limpy's mucus was dry with fear as well as diesel. He'd heard the rumors about four-wheel drives. How four-wheel drives didn't need roads. How four-wheel drives could go anywhere. But he'd thought they were just scary stories. "Eat your mashed leeches," he'd heard a mum say to some little cane toads once, "or a four-wheel drive will come and get you."

Now he knew it was true.

"Three croaks for Uncle Nick!" said Aunty Ellen.

She scraped a handful of flying insects off Uncle Nick and held them up.

"And," she added, "three even bigger croaks for Limpy and Goliath!"

The uncles and aunts and cousins and neighbors that were crowded around the edge of the swamp in the moonlight gave three hearty croaks. And a couple of burps for good luck.

Limpy tried to look pleased. He tried not to show the others how anxious he was feeling. He tried to stop straining his ears for the sound of the four-wheel drive coming back.

He looked around at his loving relatives and tried to convince himself that they were right. That the driver of the four-wheel drive wasn't a murderous cane toad hunter. That he or she had just fallen asleep and veered off the highway accidentally and had been woken up by the sound of hysterical wombats and was already back on the highway and gone forever.

Think positive, he told himself. This is a celebration. Look happy.

"Limpy got the Uncle Nick idea from watching an echidna," Goliath was telling the rellies. "You know how anteaters have sticky tongues? So the ants stick to them?"

Limpy realized the rellies were nodding and looking admiringly at him. They were waiting for him to say something.

"Goliath helped me develop the idea," said Limpy.

He decided for Goliath's sake not to go into detail. Goliath did it instead.

"Before Limpy thought of using Uncle Nick," said Goliath proudly, "I put sticky sap on my tongue."

Now the rellies were looking at Goliath admiringly.

"My tongue was even stickier than an anteater's," continued Goliath. "Actually, it was a bit too sticky. I spent last night up one of the railway-crossing light poles with my tongue stuck to the wood. Took three cousins hanging off each leg to rip me down."

Goliath poked his tongue out so everyone could see the splinters of wood.

The rellies weren't looking quite so admiring now. Some of them looked a bit ill.

Poor Goliath, thought Limpy. He was only trying his best.

"Uncle Nick and I couldn't have done it without Goliath," said Limpy. "Three croaks for Goliath!"

The rellies who weren't feeling queasy gave three more croaks.

Limpy felt a hand on his shoulder.

"Well done, son. We're proud of you."

Limpy turned, and Dad gave him a hug.

"I always knew you'd be a leader," said Dad. "When you were a tadpole and that flood washed away most of your brothers and sisters and you got wedged in that rock, I knew you were destined for great things."

"Thanks, Dad," said Limpy, throat sac trembling

with pride. "But I don't want to be a leader, I just want to keep us safe."

He saw Mum had hopped over too. She was standing there, looking down at Uncle Nick with a sad expression on her face.

Limpy realized all the flying insects had been picked off Uncle Nick and eaten. He was just about to offer to get Mum some more when she spoke first.

"Poor Uncle Nick," she said, dabbing at her eyes with a moth.

Limpy felt a pang in his guts. Was Mum upset about him and Goliath chucking one of her brothers around?

"Your Uncle Nick was a dreamer," continued Mum. "He used to spend hours gazing up at birds and planes, wishing he could fly. And now, thanks to you, Limpy, he can."

She gave Limpy a tearful kiss and hug.

"We're so lucky," she said. "Having you to keep us safe. We're the luckiest cane toads in the whole wide swamp."

Limpy enjoyed the hug for a few moments, but then found himself thinking about the four-wheel drive again.

What if it came back?

How safe would Mum and Dad and the others be then?

Standing there, watching Mum and Dad lick the last insect legs off Uncle Nick, Limpy felt his warts tingle. Suddenly he had a new plan. A plan so big and scary it made his glands ache.

He tried to pull himself together.

Stop being a jelly bug's wobbly bits, he said to himself sternly. This is urgent. You've got to tell this plan to the others now, straightaway, tonight.

Most important, you've got to tell it to Ancient Eric.

Limpy felt faint at the thought.

Ancient Eric was very scary.

Maybe not tonight, he said to himself. Tomorrow. Or next week.

He decided to have another hug with Mum. Before he could, there was a buzz of excited whispering among the relatives. The crowd parted to let someone through.

Limpy looked up.

Aunty Ellen was coming toward him. She was leading someone carefully by the hand. The relatives were all gazing in awe, even the queasy ones. Limpy saw who it was and gulped.

Ancient Eric.

Limpy could hardly believe it.

Ancient Eric never came out of his cave under the big rock. The rumor was that even moonlight was too strong for his ancient skin, which had gone completely smooth and white with age. Ancient Eric didn't like visitors either, though that wasn't so much to do with his skin as his really bad temper.

I've got to risk it, thought Limpy. I've got to tell him my plan.

As Ancient Eric got closer, Limpy opened his mouth. But no croaks came out.

"Let's get it over with," snapped Ancient Eric to Aunty Ellen. "I've got a snake stew waiting for me, and I want to get back before the snakes escape."

Aunty Ellen cleared her throat.

"Limpy and Goliath," she said. "Ancient Eric would like to say a few words."

The swamp fell silent.

Ancient Eric looked at Limpy and Goliath, then at Uncle Nick, then back at Limpy and Goliath.

Limpy could feel Goliath trembling next to him. He hoped Goliath didn't wet himself. It wasn't a good thing, doing a wee in front of someone as important as Ancient Eric.

"Well done, boys," boomed Ancient Eric. "Thanks to your ingenuity and imagination, cane toads will be able to gather flying insects in safety and live in peace, harmony, and security forever. Now where's my dinner?"

Ancient Eric started heading back toward his cave. The relatives gave three more croaks even louder than before.

Limpy took a deep breath and shouted above the din, "No, they won't!"

The swamp fell silent again. Blood drained from warty faces. Limpy heard Mum gasp. Goliath crossed his legs.

Ancient Eric turned and glared at Limpy.

"What do you mean?" he growled.

Limpy felt his throat sac go tight with stress. He opened all his skin pores to let some relaxing air in. Everyone was looking at him.

"We're not living in peace and security here," said Limpy, trying to keep his voice steady. "Humans around here hate us. That four-wheel drive earlier tonight was probably looking for cane toads to kill. It could be back tomorrow with loads of other vehicles."

Limpy heard the rellies murmuring to one another. Nobody told Ancient Eric he was wrong. Not ever.

Limpy took another deep breath. Now for the hard bit.

"I reckon," he said, "we should find a place where humans will leave us alone. And all move there."

Everyone stared at him, dumbstruck.

"It's all the excitement," said Dad apologetically to Ancient Eric. "It's overheated his brain."

Ancient Eric's eyelids drooped lower over his tired pink eyes.

"When you've lived as long as I have," he rumbled at Limpy, "you'll know that humans don't drive off the highway looking for cane toads. That human tonight was either lost or asleep or taking a shortcut."

The rellies croaked their agreement.

"On the highway's a different matter," continued Ancient Eric. "Humans will always try to kill cane toads on the highway. Always have done, always will do."

"That's right, your worship," said Goliath nervously. "That's why we have to fight back. Is it okay if I go to the highway and chuck sticks at trucks?"

Ancient Eric nodded. Goliath hopped gratefully away.

Limpy was about to warn Goliath to stay off the highway, but Ancient Eric was speaking again.

"Humans will always hate cane toads," he rumbled. "Before you were born, young Limpy, a group of human bushwalkers came through here and killed six of us with a folding chair."

Some of the older rellies shuddered.

"Humans have always hated cane toads," repeated Ancient Eric, "and they always will. There is no place where we can be completely safe from them."

Limpy took another deep breath.

"What about national parks?" he said.

The other cane toads looked at one another, puzzled.

"National parks?" they murmured.

"What do you know about national parks?" growled Ancient Eric.

"A butterfly told me," said Limpy. "My sister Charm was there too. She . . ."

Limpy broke off, a sudden thought churning his guts.

He hadn't seen Charm all night. She'd promised to help with Uncle Nick, but she hadn't turned up.

Where was she?

"Go on," snapped Ancient Eric.

Limpy struggled to push the worried thought away.

"The butterfly told us," he continued, "that national

parks are places where every living thing is protected. Where no living thing is ever shot, trapped, poisoned, stabbed, run over, blown up with bike pumps, or bashed over the head with cricket bats. Or folding chairs. I reckon we should all go and live in one."

Limpy stopped, out of breath, heart going like a dung beetle's back legs.

Nobody made a sound. Limpy glanced at the rellies. They were all staring at him, frowning doubtfully like they had when Goliath told them he could fit ninety beetles in his mouth at once and still have room for a slug.

"A fine romantic yarn," said Ancient Eric. "Butterflies are always spinning romantic yarns, trying to impress ticks. Where is this dopey insect?"

Limpy's throat sac drooped.

"Goliath ate it," he said quietly.

"I see," rumbled Ancient Eric. "Okay, son, you've wasted enough of my time. There aren't any national parks. National parks are a myth. A fantasy for feeble minds. Think about it. If national parks existed, don't you think we'd already be living in one? Nature's given you a great gift, young man. A brain bigger than a leech's entire digestive system. Start using it."

Ancient Eric turned and headed back toward his cave. "Now perhaps I can have my dinner," he muttered, "or what's left of it." He called back over his shoulder, "If anyone sees any snakes with mixed herbs on them, they're mine."

The other relatives started to drift away. Limpy saw they were giving him sad, sympathetic looks. He'd seen bog weevils get looks like that, the ones who didn't have a brain because the space was taken up with an extra bottom.

"How do you know?" Limpy wanted to yell. "How do you know there aren't any national parks?"

But he didn't, because his head was throbbing with stress and his mouth was dryer than Uncle Nick's.

"Poor love," said Mum, stroking his warts. "You're a good boy, but you do have an overactive imagination."

Limpy nodded, though he didn't agree.

"Be content with what you've done," said Dad. He pointed to Uncle Nick. "Your invention's going to make flat cane toads a thing of the past."

Limpy nodded again, though he didn't agree with that either.

Two seconds later, he was proved right.

In the distance he heard a familiar sound. He prayed it was just sticks bouncing off trucks.

But it wasn't.

It was the unmistakable sound of wheels on the highway thumping over cane toads.

"Goliath!" croaked Limpy. "Charm!"

Limpy saw something was terribly wrong even before he got to the highway.

As he scrambled through the undergrowth, he caught a glimpse of someone high above the road in the white haze of the railway-crossing light.

A small figure flying through the air.

A small figure whose every dear little wart he loved like his own.

"Charm!" he yelled frantically, and flung himself toward the highway.

What had happened? Had a vehicle smashed into his sister and flung her poor lifeless body into the air?

Limpy didn't even want to think about the possibility. He wished something would remove the horrible thought from his mind.

Something did. A large tree behind him, which he crashed into headfirst.

Limpy lay on his back, dazed and frustrated, wishing that just once he could hop somewhere at top speed without his crook leg making him go round in circles.

As soon as he was able to stand up again, he hopped a bit less fast to the edge of the highway. And stopped dead, staring in stunned disbelief.

Charm was flying through the air again.

But it wasn't a vehicle that had flung her up toward the railway-crossing light, it was Goliath.

And her body wasn't lifeless, it was kicking gleefully and covered in something that looked to Limpy very much like sticky sap.

Limpy realized other small sticky cane toads were flying, giggling, through the air as well. Squatting under the light were aunts and uncles, throwing the little cane toads up into the cloud of flying insects and catching them when they came down and throwing them back up again.

Stack me, thought Limpy desperately. They're on the highway. Don't they realize the danger they're in?

He was just about to point this out to them loudly and urgently when he noticed something.

The sticky little cane toads had flying insects stuck all over them.

A lot more flying insects, Limpy had to admit, than had been stuck to Uncle Nick.

Then Limpy felt the road start to vibrate and heard a low rumble that got rapidly louder. Headlight beams suddenly punched through the darkness, and a vehicle came speeding round the bend in the highway.

"Look out!" screamed Limpy. "A car!"

The adult cane toads, gazing up at the golden cloud of flying insects, took a moment to realize what was happening. And when they did, most of them had to wait even longer for their little airborne assistants to drop back down into their arms.

Limpy threw himself toward Goliath, hoping to catch Charm on her way down and drag them both to safety. But his crook leg gave way and he found himself hopping half a circle into the ditch.

The car roared past. Limpy buried his head in his arms, trying not to hear anything.

But he heard it anyway.

The horrible squeal of a car swerving to take aim, and the even more horrible thump-thump pop-pop of tires running over cane toads.

"Charm," moaned Limpy to himself. "Goliath."

When the car had thudded over the railway crossing and accelerated away into the night, Limpy crawled out of the ditch and squinted, trembling, at the road.

There they were, on the tarmac, just as he'd feared.

Four damp patches of pressed skin and flat warts.

Weak with distress, Limpy edged closer, wanting to see if any of them was Charm or Goliath, and yet not wanting to.

Before he could bring himself to look properly, he felt someone tugging the flap of skin next to his armpit.

He looked down.

It was Charm. She was grinning up at him, her dear little face glowing with excitement.

"Look, Limpy," she said. "I've collected enough dinner for a week."

Her sticky sap-smeared body was covered with so many flying insects it was like she had soft, multi-colored, frantically struggling fur.

Goliath was squatting proudly behind her.

"Better than Uncle Nick pizza, eh?" he grinned.

Limpy was so relieved he wanted to hug them both. He also wanted to strangle them.

"You could have been killed," he croaked. He looked weakly at the aunts and uncles, who were brushing car dust off themselves and their flying-insect-covered offspring. "You all could have been killed."

Limpy's glands ached as he imagined Charm and Goliath squished onto the highway next to the other four flat rellies. Suddenly his warts burned with anger.

"Why didn't you stick to my original plan?" he

demanded. "I worked out that Frisbee method so you wouldn't have to go onto the highway. So you wouldn't end up flatter than cow poo with your brains baking on the bitumen."

Nobody said anything. The aunts and uncles glanced at one another nervously. Limpy realized they'd probably never seen him this angry, but he didn't care.

"What maniac," he said, "came up with the idea of doing it this way? Risking everyone's lives like this just to get a few extra flying insects a bit more quickly?"

Goliath took a hop back. "It wasn't me, honest."

Limpy saw that Goliath was looking nervously up at someone or something behind Limpy.

Then Limpy felt himself being lifted off his feet by the loose skin at the back of his neck.

The other cane toads all took a respectful step back, and Limpy realized that a huge shadow had fallen over them.

"It was me," said a voice. "Do you have a problem with that?"

Limpy recognized the voice instantly. It was confident and loud, but with a soft wet hiss to it like the sound of a slug being sucked through a water rat's teeth.

Malcolm.

Limpy twisted round and found himself looking up at the biggest cane toad in the whole wide swamp.

Malcolm was staring down at him. At first Malcolm's expression looked to Limpy like fond amusement. Then Limpy spotted something else in Malcolm's eyes.

It was either hatred or indigestion.

Malcolm gripped Limpy's neck skin even tighter.

I don't think this is indigestion, thought Limpy.

He desperately tried to stop his throat sac from wobbling. He didn't want Malcolm to see he was scared.

Because he wasn't.

Not really.

Oversized wartbag, thought Limpy angrily. Just because you're big and strong and handsome and popular and both your legs work properly, that doesn't give you the right to risk the lives of innocent family members.

Limpy decided to tell Malcolm that now.

Malcolm lifted Limpy up level with his face.

Limpy gulped. Malcolm's warts were huge. Each one was as big as a medium-sized dung beetle.

Then Malcolm's eyes went cloudy, like lizard blood in water, and his face split into a smile as wide as a buffalo's bottom crack.

"So, fourth cousin," purred Malcolm. "Don't be offended, but it seemed to me that your flying-insect-gathering plan was a bit inefficient. Not to mention disrespectful to the sadly departed. So I offered these good folks my plan, which guarantees them forty-five percent more flying insects in thirty-five percent less time. Of course they accepted. I hope you don't have a problem with that."

"Actually," said Limpy, struggling to stop his voice from wavering, "I do." He pointed to the squashed rellies on the highway. "I have a problem with you getting family members killed. And I also have a problem with you risking the lives of innocent little kids."

"Hey!" said Charm indignantly. "I'm not a little kid."

Limpy saw her glance up at Malcolm and blush.

"I just haven't grown a lot," she muttered. "'Cause of pollution."

Limpy's glands stiffened. That bashful look on Charm's face. He'd seen it on other toads' faces when the night breeze was perfumed with jacaranda flowers and romance and that strong smell you get when you chew a toilet deodorant block.

Limpy's insides churned with horror.

Charm was in love with Malcolm.

Charm gave Limpy a guilty glance, then looked back up at Malcolm.

"Could you put my brother down, please?" she said.

Malcolm didn't move. Limpy saw he was looking at Charm with amusement. Charm, misty-eyed, didn't seem to care.

"Hey," said Goliath to Malcolm, pulling himself up to his full height, which was almost level with Malcolm's chest. "You heard what the lady said."

Limpy flinched as the smiling Malcolm's eyes flickered with anger.

"Um," stammered Goliath, flinching too. "What she said was that if you could please see your way clear to putting Limpy down when you have a moment, we'd all be very grateful."

Limpy felt himself falling. He hit the ground hard. His vision went blurry for a moment, but he could still hear Malcolm's voice.

"Limpy has a good heart," Malcolm was saying, "but he's weak and sentimental. If we're like him, we won't stand a chance against the humans. If, on the other hand, we're strong and determined and we have a good business plan, we can survive."

The other cane toads looked thoughtful and murmured things to one another. Limpy hoped they were planning to wedge Malcolm inside a hollow log and tickle him with hairy spiders until he apologized for being rude to fourth cousins.

"We suffered a few place mats tonight," continued Malcolm, nodding toward the squashed rellies on the road. "But that's part of being strong. Some of us must sacrifice our lives so the rest of us can have a lot more to eat."

There was a general croak of agreement from the rellies.

Limpy couldn't believe what he was hearing. He struggled to find his voice. Shock and amazement were making his mucus dry up.

"Place mats?" he croaked up at Malcolm. "These aren't place mats. These are members of our family. And why do you keep saying 'we'? I didn't see you out there on the highway risking your neck flaps."

Malcolm sighed. He reached down and pulled Limpy to his feet.

"It's not easy for you, Limpy, we understand that," said Malcolm gently. "When you were younger and that truck squashed your leg, I'm thinking it may have squashed a bit of your brain too. Which is why you don't understand some things. Like how a leader never risks his own life, because he's too valuable a resource."

"What Malcolm means," said Charm gently to Limpy, "is that he has to keep himself safe so we can all benefit from his leadership."

More croaks of agreement from the rellies.

Limpy looked up angrily at Malcolm.

"You're not our leader," he said. "Ancient Eric is. I think we should let Ancient Eric decide what's best for us."

Limpy turned and hopped unsteadily off toward Ancient Eric's cave.

Please follow me, he begged the others silently. Please don't go back onto the highway.

After a bit, he heard the others following. He slowed down to let Charm and Goliath catch up. But it wasn't either of them who appeared alongside him.

"I've been watching you, you little slug," hissed Malcolm, leaning down and spraying mucus into Limpy's ear. "Trying to impress everyone with your brave exploits and clever ideas. Well, here's some advice, son. That plan you've got to take over from Ancient Eric, forget it. I'll be taking over because I'm big and strong and you're a deformed little maggot."

Malcolm straightened up and hopped away on his huge, muscular legs.

Limpy watched him go, speechless with shock, struggling to digest what Malcolm had just said.

Me take over from Ancient Eric? thought Limpy. That's crazy. The idea's never even entered my head. Not even the time Dad was going on about how he reckoned if there was ever a cane toad prime minister of Australia, it would be me.

Charm and Goliath appeared at Limpy's side.

"Don't be too hard on Malcolm," said Charm. "He does have good ideas."

"Okay, he gets the odd little thing wrong," said Goliath. "Like your brain being squashed. I checked your ears after your accident and you didn't have a single bit of brain sticking out of them."

"Thanks," said Limpy dully.

"But you can't argue with a couple of million extra food portions," continued Goliath, running his tongue over Charm's back and scooping up a mouthful of flying insects.

"And you have to admit," said Charm, "he is pretty nice."

Limpy sighed miserably as he watched Charm and Goliath hop away and join the other cane toads hurrying after Malcolm.

"Just stay off the highway," Limpy called after them.

Charm and Goliath were already so far ahead he wasn't sure if they could hear him.

He shouted it again, but this time he knew they couldn't because his voice was drowned out by the roar of a motor.

A motor nearby.

Much closer than the highway.

Limpy spun round.

A big dark familiar shape with lights on the front crashed out of a clump of bushes, heading straight for him.

Limpy's guts turned to jelly.

The four-wheel drive was back.

Limpy did a frantic backward somersault into a tangle of creepers and wriggled down as far as he could into the dark boggy undergrowth.

The four-wheel drive roared closer.

Go back, begged Limpy. Go back to your natural habitat.

The four-wheel drive stopped.

Trembling, Limpy peered out of his hiding place.

The four-wheel drive was standing only about six wombat-lengths away, growling hungrily, its brake lights red and angry, its exhaust a ghostly vapor in the moonlight.

A jolt of terror stabbed through Limpy as a light snapped on at the front of the vehicle, even brighter than the headlights. It was a spotlight on the roof. Limpy saw a human arm reach out of the driver's window and swivel the spotlight slowly from side to side.

A big white circle of light slid across the undergrowth.

Startled centipedes and snails froze, little mouths
hanging open.

Don't worry, thought Limpy grimly. He's not after
you.

Limpy knew what this human was after. This was a
human who was prepared to drive his vehicle off the
highway and get it all muddy just so he could kill
more cane toads.

Limpy shivered.

The spotlight was moving slowly across the area
between where he was hidden and the swamp in the
distance. So far it hadn't lit up any cane toads, but
Limpy knew that Charm and Goliath were out there
somewhere. And Mum and Dad. And all the rellies.

If they stayed there, trembling in the undergrowth
like him, the spotlight would seek them out sooner or
later, and then those big fat tires would hunt them
down.

I've got to do something, thought Limpy desperately.

The cool mud against his cheek helped him think
clearly, and suddenly he had an idea.

He dragged himself out of the undergrowth, hurried round to the front of the vehicle, and hopped
into the dazzle from the spotlight.

"Hey!" he yelled. "Over here!"

Limpy knew the human couldn't understand what he was saying, so he jumped up and down and waved.

The four-wheel drive jolted into gear and started moving toward him.

Limpy turned and hopped toward the swamp.

"Stay hidden!" he yelled to the others. "I'm going to lure him into the deep part of the swamp. Even a four-wheel drive can't go far when it's up to its axles in swampweed and eel slime."

Limpy could hear the engine roar getting louder and feel the lights on his back getting hotter, and he knew the human was gaining on him.

He hopped faster.

Then the one thing he hoped wouldn't happen happened.

His crook leg gave way. Suddenly he wasn't hopping in a straight line anymore. He was curving round toward the residential end of the swamp. Desperately he tried to straighten up, but it was no good. If he didn't stop, he'd be leading a four-wheel drive through Mum's living room. All their homes would be crushed. So would any rellies hiding under the beds.

Numb with exhaustion and disappointment, Limpy threw himself onto the ground and waited for the human to drive over him.

But even as the huge thumping tires got closer,

34

Limpy saw a flash of angry red warts out of the corner of his eye and heard a familiar voice yelling.

"Over here, you mongrel!"

Goliath.

"Come on!" roared Goliath, dancing around in a fury and waving a stick at the four-wheel drive. "Catch me if you can, big bum!"

Limpy held his breath as the four-wheel drive swerved, missing him by less than the width of a non-flattened uncle, and thundered after Goliath.

Limpy raised his head and watched with shaky relief as Goliath led the vehicle toward the deep part of the swamp.

He felt like cheering, right up until Goliath tripped on a twig and disappeared headfirst down a wombat hole.

"Oh no," croaked Limpy, scrambling to his feet.

He could see other cane toads peering from their hiding places, anxious faces gleaming in the spotlight.

"Get back under cover!" yelled Limpy.

"It's okay, everyone," said another voice loudly. "I'm here now."

Limpy's mouth fell open as the massive figure of Malcolm sprang into the spotlight. Malcolm paused for a moment, flexed his perfectly formed thighs, then headed for the swamp with huge, muscular hops.

The four-wheel drive charged after him.

I don't believe it, thought Limpy as he tried to keep up. Malcolm's risking his life for us. Perhaps I've been wrong about him. Perhaps underneath all that handsomeness and ambition, he's a decent bloke after all.

Ahead, Malcolm suddenly veered to one side.

Limpy saw that Malcolm wasn't heading for the deep part of the swamp anymore; he was heading for Ancient Eric's cave.

What had happened? Had one of Malcolm's legs gone crook as well?

No, Limpy realized. Malcolm was doing this on purpose.

"Look out!" yelled Limpy, but it was too late.

As Malcolm leaped over Ancient Eric's rock, the human saw it for the first time and hit his brakes. The four-wheel drive went into a skid and slammed into the rock.

The sound of the impact echoed across the swamp.

Then silence, except for the chugging of the engine.

Limpy wondered if the human was dead. He kept on wondering this as he crept warily toward the still vehicle.

Until, slowly, the driver's door started to open.

Limpy looked around in alarm. Rellies and family members were emerging from their hiding places, clearly visible in the moonlight.

I've got to distract the human, thought Limpy. Stop him from seeing all the others.

Limpy flung himself forward.

Then he spotted Malcolm in the shadows near the vehicle.

Perhaps Malcolm was having the same idea.

But it wasn't Malcolm who hopped toward the pair of feet that were emerging from the driver's door.

It was Charm.

Limpy saw Malcolm give her a little push and Charm look up at him adoringly, then turn and hop bravely toward the feet.

Limpy couldn't believe it. The wartbag was sacrificing Charm to save his own skin.

"No!" yelled Limpy.

He lunged forward and somehow managed to get to the feet first, so it was his body the warm human fingers closed around instead of Charm's.

Limpy felt himself being lifted high into the air.

Defiantly he looked at his captor.

And felt his poison glands go wobbly with relief.

The human had a beard and was wearing a khaki shirt and shorts.

It was plumage Limpy recognized. He'd seen photos of similar humans in magazines chucked from passing cars. He'd watched blokes like this one in action on portable tellies in human campsites. He'd heard koalas whisper dreamily about this wonderful plumage after they'd eaten too many gum leaves.

He's a conservationist, thought Limpy happily. He hasn't come to kill us, he's come to save us.

Even though Limpy was out of breath, he tried to yell that to the others, and kept trying until he saw the big gleaming needle in the human's other hand and felt it jab into his tummy warts and everything went black.

"Ouch," said Limpy.

Daylight was stinging his eyeballs.

Something else was stinging his back. Worse than stinging, hurting. He hadn't felt pain like it for years, not since the truck had run over his leg.

I don't get it, thought Limpy. Why's my back hurting? The needle went into my tummy, not my back.

A horrible thought hit him. Perhaps it was a fork wound. Perhaps the human had tried to eat him while he was unconscious.

Would a conservationist do that? Limpy hoped not, for all their sakes. But his back was killing him.

What had happened?

Limpy tried to look over his shoulder, but that only made the pain worse.

I need a mirror, he thought.

He looked around, but all he could see was blue

plastic. No puddles, no shiny metal, no spare lizard eyeballs, no reflective surfaces of any kind.

Just smooth curved plastic walls.

Stack me, thought Limpy. I'm in a bucket.

He knew he should be scared, but his back was hurting too much for that.

I know, thought Limpy, grimacing. I'll do a wee and look at my back in that.

Before he did, he glanced up in case the bucket happened to be standing close to a side-view mirror on the four-wheel drive.

It wasn't. The bucket was half under what looked to Limpy like a folding table, the kind humans used for picnics and washing toddlers on after they fell into mud holes.

"Ouch," said Limpy again. Tilting his head was making his back hurt even more.

But suddenly he didn't care. Above him he saw, hanging over the edge of the picnic table and clearly visible against the sky and the trees, several large sheets of paper covered in squiggly lines and colored patches.

Maps.

Limpy knew what maps were because he'd seen people using them in cars. Maps were what humans used to find places and start arguments.

Places like, for example, national parks.

Limpy's warts tingled with excitement.

Perhaps that's why the conservationist captured me, he thought. Perhaps it's part of a plan to transport all cane toads to the safety of national parks.

Limpy was wondering how he could arrange for Charm and Goliath and Mum and Dad and the other rellies to go to the same national park as him when a drop of something wet plopped onto his head.

Rain?

For a breathless moment, Limpy pictured the bucket filling up with rain and his floating to the top and escaping and rounding up the family so they could all travel together.

Then he tasted the trickle running down his cheek.

It wasn't water, it was saliva.

Limpy looked up.

A face was staring down at him. A big face with floppy ears and sad eyes and a droopy wet mouth.

For a second Limpy thought the conservationist had shaved off his beard during the night.

Then he realized it was a dog.

"Good," said the dog, without any enthusiasm that Limpy could hear. "You've woken up at last. We thought you'd carked it."

I still might, thought Limpy grimly, if my back's anything to go by.

"Not much fun, these conservation projects, are they?" said the dog mournfully.

Limpy wondered how much the dog knew about what was going on. Maybe the dog was the conservationist's assistant. Humans would probably prefer dog assistants because they could kill their own fleas whereas human assistants, so Limpy had heard, needed chemical sprays.

"I'll get the boss," said the dog.

"No, wait," said Limpy. "I want to ask you something. Are there any national parks around here?"

The dog thought for a moment.

"Yeah. Over to the east. Huge. Can't miss it."

Limpy felt like doing a cartwheel. Then he remembered his back. Plus he still had to ask the six-million-mudworm question.

"This conservation project," said Limpy. "Does it involve transporting cane toads to national parks where we can live safely and happily for ever and ever?"

The dog thought for another moment.

"No," said the dog flatly. "It involves infecting cane toads with a virus that'll kill you all."

Limpy felt weak with shock. He stared up at the dog, desperately hoping the dog wasn't speaking in an official capacity after all.

"We did it to rabbits," continued the dog. "Got rid of millions. Once a few were infected, they passed the germs on to the others. We're not sure if the cane toad virus will work as well as that. Still experimenting. If you want more details, see the boss; he's the scientist. Oh well, nice to talk, but I'd better give him a yell."

The dog disappeared.

Limpy's head was reeling with fear and panic.

He hung on to one thought.

Must warn the others.

Ignoring the pain in his back, Limpy flung himself up the side of the bucket. It was no good. He couldn't grip. The plastic was too slippery. As he slid down for the hundredth time, a shadow fell over the bucket.

The scientist, still with his beard, peered in.

"Good on you, little fella," said the scientist. "With us at last."

Limpy couldn't understand the language, but he was pretty sure he knew what the scientist had said: Now that my dopey assistant has spilled the beans, I'm going to have to kill you.

Limpy lay miserably in the bottom of the bucket while the scientist carried it into the bush. He didn't want to die, but he'd gladly do it ten times over if he could warn the others first.

Limpy felt the bucket tip up, and he rolled out onto soft mud. He thought of hopping for it, but he knew it would be no good.

The spade or the cricket bat would be crashing down onto him any second.

Bye, Charm, he thought sadly. Bye, Goliath. Stay off the highway.

The spade still hadn't come.

Thanks, Mum, he added. Thanks, Dad. I really appreciated all the love and peeled slugs.

Still no spade. Or folding chair.

Limpy, trembling, heard the scientist say something.

"Okay, little fella, now do your job."

Limpy didn't understand the words, but he knew what they meant.

Prepare to die.

Then he heard an amazing sound. The scientist walking back toward his camp, whistling.

Limpy lay very still, mind racing.

Had the scientist gone to get a gun? Or a large rock? Or was he planning to use the four-wheel drive? Or a bike pump?

Limpy squirmed into the mud. He hoped he'd be harder to see there than hopping in circles.

He listened to the scientist pack up the camp.

He listened to the scientist drive away.

Into the distance.

Onto the highway.

Silence.

Limpy staggered to his feet.

I don't get it, he thought. I'm still alive. The scientist has let me go.

Why?

It didn't matter. The important thing was, he could warn the others.

With a surge of relief, Limpy headed toward the swamp. There was still time. He could get everyone packed up and off to a national park before the scientist started his plan. . . .

Limpy stopped.

He remembered the needle the scientist had injected him with.

He remembered what the dog had said about infecting a few rabbits and their passing the germs on to the others.

Suddenly Limpy felt sicker than he'd ever felt before.

Not just because of the pain in his back where, he realized now, the germ needle must have gone right through him.

And not just because of the millions of germs that even now must be swimming through his veins.

Because of something far worse.

Limpy's glands and warts and throat sac ached with anguish.

Whatever I do, he thought, I mustn't pass the virus germs on to Mum and Dad and Charm and Goliath.

Which means I'll have to stay away from them for ever and ever.

Limpy knew all about crying because he'd seen humans and car windshields do it.

Now, crouched behind the sticky sap tree, gazing sadly across the clearing at his dear family, Limpy felt like doing it too.

He tried to stop himself. Crying blurred your vision, especially when your tears were made of mucus. Limpy didn't want eyes full of slime, not now, not when he was looking at Charm and Goliath and Mum and Dad for what was probably the last time.

But he couldn't help it.

Afterward, when he'd wiped his eyes, Limpy saw the family were all crying too. They were gathered at the edge of the swamp with all the other rellies, and everyone was sniffling and dabbing at their eyes with dry bark or furry caterpillars.

What's happened? wondered Limpy. Have they heard about the germs already?

He wished he could go and give them a goodbye hug and tell them they'd be okay as long as they went straight to the national park and didn't kiss any strange cane toads.

I don't dare, thought Limpy. Even if I stick a big leaf over my nose and mouth, it's too risky. One sneeze or cough and I could infect everyone.

He didn't dare go even a bit closer. If virus germs were anything like wild pig fleas, they could probably jump huge distances even without wild pigs chasing them.

All he could do was stay hidden and watch.

Then Limpy saw something that made him feel even more miserable: Malcolm putting one big arm round Charm and the other round Mum, as if he was taking care of them.

"Get your paws off my family," muttered Limpy.

He wanted to shout it, but he didn't in case they might hear and come hurrying over. He watched in frustration as Malcolm took one of Mum's hands and started patting it.

"Yuck," groaned Limpy.

Virus germs or no virus germs, Limpy could barely stop himself from rushing across the clearing and jamming a sharp twig up Malcolm's nose. In fact, he knew he couldn't stop himself, not unless he did something drastic.

He did something drastic.

He hopped round to the front of the sticky sap tree, then flung himself back against it. The sticky sap gripped him all the way from his neck to his buttocks.

Malcolm was giving Dad's shoulder a sympathetic squeeze.

Limpy struggled to free himself, to get over there and sort Malcolm out with a large lump of possum poo, but the sticky sap held him tight.

Where's Ancient Eric? thought Limpy furiously. Ancient Eric should be the one helping everyone get over the scare of the four-wheel drive, not smarmy-mucus Malcolm.

Limpy watched as Malcolm went over to a small mound of earth, turned, puffed out his chest, and addressed the gathered rellies.

"Ancient Eric was a fine leader," he intoned, "and we will always remember him."

What?

Limpy strained to hear more.

Malcolm bent forward and placed something on the mound of earth. It was flat and white and very smooth.

Limpy gasped.

It was Ancient Eric.

Squashed.

But how? Ancient Eric hadn't been near the highway since cars got power steering.

Then Limpy remembered how Malcolm had changed direction and made the four-wheel drive crash into Ancient Eric's rock. Ancient Eric must have come out of his cave to see what all the racket was about just before the moment of impact and been squashed. Talk about tragic timing.

Unless . . .

It was a terrible thought, and Limpy's warts burned as he had it.

Unless Malcolm had planned it that way.

"It is with gratitude and humility," Malcolm was saying solemnly now to the other cane toads, "that I accept your invitation to take his place as your leader."

Limpy felt like his warts were going to explode. He kicked and wriggled, flailing his arms, trying to tear himself off the tree so he could hop across the clearing in a huge furious semicircle and tell everyone what Malcolm had done.

But all Limpy managed to do was get one of his hands stuck to the tree as well.

Malcolm was still speaking. What Limpy heard next made him jolt with shock so violently that his hand ripped away from the tree.

"Limpy was much loved by us all," said Malcolm,

"and we will always remember him. He was a close personal friend of mine, even though he was a bit pushy at times."

Was?

Limpy stared across the clearing.

Malcolm was standing next to another mound of earth.

Mum and Dad and Charm and Goliath were sobbing so hard now, Limpy could see their shoulders shaking even at that distance.

Stack me, thought Limpy, stunned. They think I'm dead too.

"In the absence of Limpy's body," Malcolm was saying, "which after a thorough search of the area we've failed to locate and which we assume was taken by the human to be made into a handbag or something, Limpy's family would like to commemorate him with some of his things."

Limpy watched in anguish as Mum and Dad and Charm and Goliath moved unsteadily forward one by one and gently placed familiar objects on his grave.

His collection of soft drink cans.

His newspaper and magazine scraps.

His sun-dried chicken bones.

All the precious things he'd collected that had been chucked from passing vehicles.

Limpy couldn't stand it. His poor dear family,

racked with grief and misery. Suffering all that pain over his death when he wasn't even dead.

Yet.

Desperately, Limpy struggled to free himself from the sticky sap. He had to let them know he was still alive. Then he remembered the virus germs and stopped struggling.

It's better this way, he thought. If they think I'm dead, they won't come looking for me and put themselves at risk.

But it wasn't that much better. They were still in danger from the scientists, and Limpy couldn't even warn them.

"Now that," said a voice, "is bad luck."

Limpy looked around.

"You reckon you're unlucky," said the voice. "Just because your folks think you're dead and you're not. That's not unlucky. This is unlucky."

Limpy felt something tickling him and looked down and saw that the voice belonged to a flying beetle that had got stuck to the back of his hand.

"One cane toad in fifty million square kilometers with sticky sap on his fist," said the beetle, "and I fly into it. Okay. That much bad luck you can't beat. I give up. Eat me."

Limpy stared at the beetle. Suddenly he had an idea that made his warts light up.

"Tell you what," said Limpy. "If you'll do something for me, I won't eat you."

"Anything," said the beetle. "As long as it doesn't involve selling cigarettes to children."

Limpy pointed across the clearing at Goliath. "See that big cane toad?" he said. "Not the really big one with the smug expression, the fairly big one sobbing and trying to console himself with a mouthful of bog worms. I want you to give him a message."

The beetle nodded.

"Tell him," said Limpy, "that all cane toads are in great danger and that he must get everybody away from Malcolm and head east and find the national park as quickly as possible."

"Right," said the beetle. "Danger, away from Malcolm, east, national park. Shall I say who the message is from?"

"Tell him it's from Limpy," said Limpy quietly. "Say I gave you the message just before I died."

The beetle gave Limpy a strange look.

"Okeydoke," said the beetle. "You're the one not eating me."

Limpy carefully unstuck the beetle from his hand. The beetle hovered in front of Limpy's face for a moment, beaming with gratitude.

"Boy," he said. "This is my lucky day."

Limpy didn't take his eyes off the beetle as it flew

across the clearing. For a brief moment he thought it was going to Malcolm by mistake, but it veered away and hovered in front of Goliath.

"Give him the message," whispered Limpy. "Give him the message."

He saw Goliath spot the beetle and look pleasantly surprised and lean forward close enough to hear what the beetle was about to say.

Limpy sighed with relief.

Then Goliath's tongue shot out and the beetle vanished into his mouth.

Limpy didn't take his eyes off the twenty-sixth beetle as it flew across the clearing.

The beetle reached Goliath and hovered in front of him.

Limpy whispered the words he'd whispered twenty-five times before.

"Give him the message."

Before the beetle could speak, Goliath looked amazed at his own repeated good fortune and his tongue shot out for the twenty-sixth time.

"No," groaned Limpy.

He gave up trying to get a message to his family.

For a while he slumped dejectedly, his back throbbing painfully against the sticky bark of the tree. Then he noticed something else happening across the clearing. Malcolm was unfolding a map and holding it up in front of the assembled cane toads.

Limpy stared. It looked like one of the scientist's maps. How had Malcolm got it?

"Attention, everyone!" said Malcolm. "We will be leaving for our new home at sunset."

Limpy's mouth fell open. What was going on? Had Malcolm heard about the national park? Was he going to lead the cane toads there?

Glands twitching hopefully, Limpy squinted across the clearing, trying to see exactly where Malcolm was pointing on the map. It was no good. Goliath kept pulling big creepers down in front of the map and sucking leeches off them.

"I will lead you to a place," Malcolm was saying, "where cane toads can live in peace and safety forever."

Yes, thought Limpy, warts tingling with relief.

He watched the assembled rellies discuss this among themselves. Most of them still looked numb from the shock of the four-wheel drive and the sadness of the funerals. Even so, they seemed pretty keen on the idea. All except Goliath, but he probably just had indigestion.

A voice rang out. "What direction are we going, Mighty Malcolm?"

Limpy smiled sadly. It was Dad.

"East," murmured Limpy to himself.

"West," said Malcolm.

"Eh?" said Limpy.

55

"Far over the horizon where the sun sets," continued Malcolm, beaming at the rellies. "I call it Sunset Estates. You'll love it. A real slice of cane toad paradise. And because you're all family, I'll be making your new homesites available at low, low discount prices, easy weekly repayments, flying insects accepted."

Limpy's throat sac was rigid with shock.

He struggled to digest what he'd just heard.

Malcolm was taking everyone in the wrong direction. To the west. Where, Limpy had heard from very thirsty galahs, the heat was crippling and swamps were nonexistent. And then, worst of all, the big wart-bag was charging everyone to live there. They'd have to spend the rest of their days risking their lives on the highway to get the flying insects to pay him. Scientists with needles full of deadly germs wouldn't even have to leave the road to get to them.

Limpy struggled to unstick himself from the sticky sap tree. It was the only thing stopping him from rushing across the clearing and confronting Malcolm and begging everyone not to go.

And, thought Limpy desolately as he stopped struggling, infecting them all.

He was still stuck to the tree hours later when Malcolm led a meandering column of rellies out of the swamp in the direction of the setting sun.

Limpy looked sadly across the clearing at Mum and Dad as they hopped after Malcolm, their tearful warty faces turned back toward home.

Charm was further ahead, next to Malcolm, but she was looking back tearfully too.

Suddenly Mum let out a cry. She broke away from the others and frantically retraced her steps and flung herself across one of the mounds of earth.

It was, Limpy realized, his grave.

"I don't want to go," sobbed Mum. "I don't want to leave my son. I don't want to leave my home."

Dad came over and gently pulled her to her feet.

"Come on," he said. "There's nothing for us here now except terrible memories."

He started leading her away. She broke free again and darted back to the grave and, Limpy saw, grabbed his favorite soft drink can.

"They're not all terrible memories," said Mum.

This time, hugging the can, she let Dad lead her back to the others.

Malcolm stood at the head of the column, watching impatiently. "Can we go now?" he said.

Charm glared angrily up at him. "Hey," she said. "We're leaving the home we love. Don't rush us."

Limpy watched Malcolm turn away from Charm and the others and roll his eyes. Then, telling the others to keep up, he led them off toward the setting sun.

Limpy felt a spasm of pain.

Not in his back, in his guts.

"Goodbye," he whispered to them all.

For a second Limpy thought Goliath was waving, but then he remembered they didn't even know he was there. Goliath must just have been trying to snatch a few stink beetles for the trip.

"Take care," whispered Limpy as his family disappeared into the dying light.

He didn't cry this time.

Not now that he knew what he had to do.

Limpy discovered it wasn't easy, peeing up his own back. Especially since the sun had gone down and he was having to aim in the dark. He got the hang of it eventually, though, and after a while the sticky sap started to dissolve.

He staggered away from the tree and went and lay in the swamp for a while to wash off the rest of the sap and soothe his aching warts.

Then he visited Ancient Eric.

As Limpy approached the moonlit mound of earth, he heard a hissing sound.

For a scary moment Limpy thought Malcolm had come back to get something he'd forgotten. His map or his exercise equipment. Then Limpy saw it was just a couple of snakes with dried herbs on them, chortling at poor Ancient Eric.

"Not so hungry now, eh, flat-face?" chuckled one of the snakes.

"Come on, you miserable old windbag," hissed the other. "Eat us."

Limpy's glands prickled with anger. He was very tempted to give them a squirt. Then he remembered what Dad had told him: Don't waste your poison pus unless you're actually being attacked. Or unless you're prime minister and your press secretary tries to trim your warts off.

Limpy cleared his throat.

The snakes twitched in alarm, glowered resentfully at Limpy, and slithered away.

Limpy looked down at Ancient Eric.

It was one of the saddest sights he'd ever seen. A once-proud leader, flattened. And worse, with skin so smooth he looked like a human dinner plate with a grumpy mouth and surprised eyes.

Oh well, thought Limpy. At least the poor thing can't catch anything from me.

"Mr. Eric," said Limpy. "Things are pretty crook at the moment. I know there's nothing you can do, so I'm going to have a crack at saving everyone myself. I may not have much time left, but if I can find that national park to the east, perhaps I can rescue the others from Malcolm and get them safely there."

Loud hissing and chortling came from the nearby shadows.

"Fat chance," said the snakes. "He's kidding himself. What an idiot."

Limpy ignored them. He leaned forward and gripped Ancient Eric by the edges.

"Sorry about this," said Limpy. "I know I'm not meant to touch you, you being so important. But you need a final resting place where you won't be pestered. I think you'll find it's more dignified under my bed."

Limpy heaved Ancient Eric onto his shoulders. Ignoring the pain from his back, he hopped slowly round the edge of the swamp till he reached a familiar front path.

It didn't feel good, being in the place with everyone gone. Okay, not quite everyone. The flat sun-dried rellies were still there, aunts stacked in one corner of Limpy's room, uncles in another, cousins at the foot of his bed.

Limpy put Ancient Eric reverently into a pizza box and slid him under the bed. Then Limpy said goodbye to the flat rellies. It took a while because he wanted to do it individually and some of them were stuck together.

Finally he finished and went outside.

Limpy paused, gazing at the dear swamp he loved

so much. In the moonlight, the still water and lovely weeds were full of shadows.

And memories.

They flooded through him.

Dad teaching him not to eat giant mangrove slugs while they were kissing because if you swallowed two at a time they got stuck in your throat.

Goliath gobbling stinkweed until he had wind so bad he could speed through the water without using his arms or legs.

Mum telling Limpy and Charm that the swamp would always be their home, as long as Goliath didn't pollute the water too much.

Limpy shook his head sadly and sent the memories back into the darkness.

Would he ever see his dear home again? Would he ever know such love and happiness again?

Probably not, thought Limpy.

But there wasn't time to hang around feeling sorry for himself.

He had a train to catch.

Limpy crouched in the grass next to the train tracks and smeared sticky sap onto his knees and tummy and forehead.

"That won't make much difference," said a nearby centipede.

Limpy didn't answer.

He thought the centipede was probably right, but when you were going to fling yourself at a train moving faster than a stampeding goanna, you needed all the help you could get.

A loud whistle shrieked in the distance.

The centipede put quite a few hands over its ears.

Limpy tensed.

As the light on the front of the train hurtled toward him out of the darkness, he tried to think of positive things.

How the train would almost certainly slow down as it went over the highway crossing.

How his back wasn't hurting so much now, more sort of itching. And that might just have been from when he'd stretched the skin trying to pull himself away from the sticky sap tree.

Then the mud under Limpy's feet started to tremble and the metal tracks hummed and suddenly the train was thundering through the crossing and past Limpy.

Not slowing down at all.

"Jump!" screamed the centipede.

Limpy jumped.

For a while he thought he was dead. Arms and legs ripped off and head bouncing into the centipede's front yard.

When he realized he was still in one piece, he knew that at the very least he must be completely flat, with his face peering out of his own bottom and his brains leaking out of his ears.

So he was pretty surprised when he discovered he wasn't.

Stack me, thought Limpy. I'm still toad-shaped.

Gradually he realized the deafening noise wasn't broken bones rattling around inside him, it was the wheels of the train clattering along the tracks just below his head.

He was clinging, he saw in the moonlight flickering through the train above him, to a rusty metal beam at the bottom of one of the carriages.

But not for long.

As he and the train hurtled forward, the rush of air was tearing him off the beam. Even though he was clinging on as hard as he could with both arms and his good leg, he could feel himself sliding painfully across the rust.

The sticky sap was useless. The wind had already turned it into a dry, flaky film on his chest. It was crumbling faster than the rust.

I've got to get off this beam, thought Limpy desperately.

He looked around. Above him and a bit behind him was a gap between the floorboards of the carriage.

It wasn't a big gap.

It was more of an Uncle Nick–sized gap.

But it was all there was.

Limpy let go of the beam, flinging his arms upward.

The wind slammed him backward.

As he became airborne, he rammed his hands through the gap and grabbed the edge of a floorboard.

Slowly, painfully, he dragged himself up into the carriage. He could feel the wind tearing at his legs and lower body. As he wriggled through the gap, the rough wood scraped flakes of sap off his skin. Then it scraped off flakes of skin.

Finally he was inside, lying trembling and exhausted on the floor of the carriage.

Safe.

Limpy gave a weary sigh of relief.

And saw, above him, about a hundred pairs of eyes, white and unblinking in the darkness.

Limpy froze. Even his trembling bits stopped moving.

Too late. The eyes were all looking at him.

"Hmmm," said a voice. "We seem to have a traveling companion."

I'm done for, thought Limpy. It's a packed tourist train. There's nothing humans on holiday like more than practicing their golf or tennis on a cane toad.

He waited for the swish of a club or a racquet, or a trail bike if the human was into motorcross.

It didn't come.

The only thing that struck Limpy was a thought.

Wait a minute! he said to himself. I understood the voice, so these can't be humans.

At that moment the train swung round a curve and moonlight spilled into the carriage.

Limpy looked around nervously.

Staring down at him were a large number of sheep.

"G'day," said Limpy, desperately trying to remember if he'd ever heard stories of sheep savaging cane toads.

He didn't think he had. Not unless some of the four-wheel drives on the highway with dark tinted windows had sheep driving them.

"Evening," said the nearest sheep. "Going far?"

"To the national park," said Limpy. "If I can find it. I know it's in this direction."

The sheep turned to the other sheep. "Any of you know where the national park is?"

The other sheep shook their heads.

"Sorry we can't be more help," said the sheep to Limpy. "Hope you find it."

"Thanks," said Limpy. "What about you? Are you on holiday?"

"Not really," said the sheep. "We're on our way to the slaughterhouse. To be killed and eaten by humans."

Limpy stared.

That was awful.

"Come with me," he said. "To the national park. All living things are protected there. Nobody will be able to eat you there, not if you don't want them to."

"Thanks," said the sheep. "But it wouldn't work. This is a locked carriage. At the other end we're put into a locked truck. And taken to a locked slaughter-house. Anyway, we've always known this is what would happen. We're, I dunno, sort of used to the idea."

Limpy looked around at their placid faces with only a hint of sadness in their big soft eyes.

Stack me! he thought angrily.

As the train raced through the night, Limpy tried to persuade the sheep to let him rescue them and take them to a life of freedom and frolic in the national park.

It was no good. They were polite but firm.

Finally, sadly, Limpy gave up.

The conversation sort of petered out after that. Limpy didn't think it was fair to keep on about the wonders of life in the national park, the brilliant mud slides and the stunning views and the fragrant bogs, not to traveling companions who'd soon be chops and sausages.

The train had been slowing down for some time, and now it jolted to a stop.

Limpy peered through a crack in the carriage wall.

When his eyes got used to the sunlight, he saw a concrete platform with rows of metal fences.

"End of the line," said one of the sheep. "Good luck. Hope you find the national park."

Limpy looked around sadly at their kind faces.

He didn't know what to say. What could you say to traveling companions who'd be ending up as roast dinners?

Hope the gravy's not too hot?

It didn't seem right, so he just gave them a grateful smile and said "Thanks."

As he squeezed through the crack in the carriage floor, he remembered something.

The virus germs.

Oh no, he thought. What if I've infected the sheep?

That wouldn't be fair, his new friends having to spend their last precious hours worrying about their health.

Then Limpy realized he was being an idiot. Humans wouldn't want to spread germs to every living animal, because if they did, they wouldn't have anything left to eat for lunch. The virus germs must just affect cane toads.

That's a relief, thought Limpy, though it wasn't much of one.

Limpy dropped onto the rusty beam under the train and looked around.

His warts prickled with fear.

Human feet in big work boots were clomping along the platform. Human feet he'd have to get past to find the national park.

Limpy looked around some more.

What he really wanted was a tunnel that led under the platform and under all the other scary human places outside and came up right in the middle of the national park, wherever it was—preferably next to a swamp.

He couldn't see one.

Which meant he'd have to go across the platform.

Limpy took a deep breath. He waited till none of the human feet were directly in front of him, made sure he had plenty of mucus so his lips wouldn't dry out when he was hopping for his life, and hopped for his life.

The bright morning sun hurt his eyes. He couldn't see if any boots were aiming for him. All he could do was head toward the patch of shade on the other side of the platform.

Not too fast, he reminded himself. If you start going in a curve you'll end up somewhere fatal, like the ladies' toilets.

Limpy felt his mucus drying up with the effort and the stress. He dreaded hearing that horrible cry humans give when they see a cane toad. The one that sounds like they've got a bog worm stuck in their throat and they don't like the taste.

The cry didn't come.

Limpy threw himself into the shade, gasping gratefully.

And saw to his relief that he was on a concrete ramp that led down into darkness. Could this be the tunnel he'd hoped for?

An ant was trotting toward him up the ramp. Followed, Limpy saw, by a swarm of other ants.

"Excuse me," Limpy said to the first ant. "Is this the way to the national park?"

"Rack off, wart-head," scowled the ant as he hurried past. "We've got a train to catch."

Limpy was tempted to have breakfast, but the ants' red bodies and red faces and red angry eyes didn't look that appetizing.

"Thanks for your help," muttered Limpy. "Have a nice day."

He turned away and headed toward the mouth of the tunnel. Before he reached it, he heard a loud cry behind him. Not, Limpy saw with relief as he spun round, from a human. From a sheep.

The sheep were being herded by the humans out of the train carriages and down wooden chutes. The first few sheep had frozen in horror and were staring at the approaching ants.

"Arghh!" screamed one of them. "Fire ants!"

Limpy watched, stunned, as the sheep tried to scramble back up the chutes in panic. Then they bolted. The humans were knocked sideways as a tide of frenzied sheep thundered across the platform. Toward, Limpy saw, his own panic rising, him.

Limpy spun back round desperately. He was trapped. Concrete walls rose up on both sides, too high to climb. Ahead was the tunnel, but soon it would be full of a frenzied stampeding mob.

Stack me, thought Limpy, weak with terror. I'm going to be trampled to death by sheep.

Then a voice rang out above him.

"Limpy. Grab my arm."

A familiar voice.

Limpy looked up. And even though the pounding sheep feet were only meters away, he froze in amazement.

"Goliath!" he yelled, weak now for different reasons. Relief and quite a bit of delight.

"Grab my arm!" shouted Goliath, hanging off the concrete wall and reaching down toward Limpy.

"Yes!" yelled Limpy. "I'm grabbing, I'm grabbing. Stack me, am I glad to see you!"

He lunged up toward Goliath's arm.

Then, delight turning to anguish, Limpy remembered something.

The virus germs.

He pulled his arm away from Goliath's.

"No!" yelled Limpy above the thunder of the sheep. "Go away!"

Goliath didn't go away.

Limpy felt muscular fingers grab the loose skin at the back of his neck. Suddenly he was dragged up the wall. Dust and wool and sheep saliva tickled his feet as the mob charged under him into the tunnel.

"Please," Limpy begged Goliath. "You mustn't touch me."

Goliath didn't seem to hear. He heaved Limpy onto the top of the wall, put his arm round him, and jumped with him down behind some wooden crates.

"We'll be safe here till the panic's over," said Goliath.

No you won't, thought Limpy miserably, pulling away. You'll never be safe again. I've probably just infected you with virus germs.

Limpy could hear the sheep bursting noisily out of

the other end of the tunnel and milling around, with humans shouting at them.

I should be down there, he said to himself, glands aching with anguish. Flattened to a pulp by hundreds of sheep feet. At least I wouldn't have done this to poor Goliath.

Goliath was grinning at him.

"Stack me, you look pale," said Goliath. "Must be the shock of seeing me. I'm pretty amazed I made it here myself."

"Goliath . . . ," croaked Limpy.

The sooner Goliath knew, the better. Perhaps if Goliath lay down and put his feet up, the germs wouldn't affect him so badly.

Wouldn't kill him so quickly.

"There's something I have to tell you," whispered Limpy.

Goliath wasn't listening.

"Talk about good luck," he was saying. "You know those flying beetles you sent over to me yesterday? I mustn't have chewed one of them properly, 'cause it crawled back up my throat and gave me your message. About you saying you were dead when you weren't really. Stack me, I thought. If Limpy's saying that, he must still be alive. So I went looking for you. Couple of snakes with herbs on them told me where you'd gone. When I heard you were definitely still alive, I was delirious. Nearly choked on the snakes. Got to the train just as you were jumping on and hopped on the back myself."

"Goliath . . . ," said Limpy.

Goliath threw his arms round Limpy again. "You don't have to say it," he said. "I know you're tickled pink, and I am too. Tickled pink you're still alive and tickled even pinker I can go on a quest with you instead of that oversized wartbag Malcolm."

Limpy couldn't get a word out, partly because Goliath was hugging him so hard and partly because he felt so sad.

I've got the most loving cousin in the universe, thought Limpy, and I may have just killed him.

Limpy wanted to cry and never stop.

Instead, he pulled himself together.

It could be worse, he thought. I could have infected Charm as well.

Limpy struggled out of Goliath's arms and was about to break the awful news when he saw what was on Goliath's back.

A shiny pink plastic backpack.

Limpy recognized it. He remembered the day a child having a tantrum in a passing car had pulled the backpack off her doll and chucked it out onto the highway. Limpy had waited for the car to turn round and come back, and when it didn't, he'd added the backpack to his drink can and chicken bone collection.

Now he stared at it in amazement.

Partly because Goliath had managed to squeeze it over his broad shoulders and partly because it was moving.

Something inside it was wriggling and kicking and grunting.

Stack me, thought Limpy. He's brought a bag full of bog worms to eat on the trip.

He saw that Goliath was glancing nervously over his shoulder at the bag.

"I was gunna explain about this," said Goliath, pulling the bag off his back. He put it gently down and undid the flap. "What happened was . . ."

He was interrupted by a roar of fury from inside the bag. The flap flew open and an irate face appeared, glaring at Goliath.

Limpy stared in stunned horror.

"Charm," he croaked, backing away. "No."

"Mongrel!" yelled Charm at Goliath. "Kidnapper!"

She clambered out of the bag and advanced furiously toward Goliath. Then she caught sight of Limpy and screamed with delight.

"Limpy!"

She started coming toward him, an amazed grin on her little face.

Limpy backed away.

"Incredible," said Charm. "You're alive! Goliath was telling the truth. I thought he abducted me 'cause he was jealous of my feelings for Malcolm."

Limpy was desperately trying to get further away from Charm, for her sake, but the wooden crate at his back was stopping him.

"Of course I was telling the truth," said Goliath indignantly. "When I worked out that Limpy was still alive, I knew he'd need our help. So I had to get you away from Mr. Handsome. Who I don't reckon is so perfect, if you want to know. I reckon some of those warts are fake. Dried dung beetles with the legs pulled off."

Charm grabbed the pink bag and tried to swing it at Goliath's head.

"Why didn't you talk to me?" she yelled. "Instead of kidnapping me. It wasn't like I was so dopey over Malcolm I wouldn't have listened."

Goliath looked pleadingly over at Limpy for help.

While Limpy was trying to work out what to do, Charm's shoulders slumped and her face slowly scrunched into a frown. "All right, I was a bit dopey," she muttered. Then her face lit up again. "Oh, Limpy, I'm so happy you're alive."

Before Limpy could stop her, she hopped over, stretched up, and kissed him.

"No," groaned Limpy. "No."

Charm stared at him, stunned and concerned.

"Limpy," she said. "What's the matter?"

"It's okay, Limpy," said Goliath. "She's your sister. It's not yucky when you kiss your sister."

"It's not that," said Limpy.

Miserably he showed them his back.

"Sort of a lumpy scab," said Goliath. "I think it looks quite nice."

Limpy told them about the scientist and the needle and the virus germs.

There was a long silence.

"Oh no," breathed Charm.

"I'm sorry," whispered Limpy.

"Virus germs?" roared Goliath. "I'm not gunna let any virus germs kill my family. I'm gunna pulverize them. I'm gunna rip their little legs off. I'm gunna eat them."

Charm put her hand on Goliath's arm.

Limpy watched Goliath's shoulders slump. Charm and Goliath exchanged a long worried look.

"I don't feel infected," said Goliath. "I just feel hungry. Do you think virus germs can make you feel hungry?"

There was another long silence.

Then Charm spoke.

"It's not your fault, Limpy," she said. "If we are

infected, I reckon we should make the most of the time we've got left. I reckon we should find the national park and do everything we can to get Mum and Dad and the others safely there before we die."

"I agree," said Goliath.

Limpy looked at their determined faces and wished cane toads gave each other those round metal things that humans gave each other for being brave.

He'd give Charm and Goliath a hundred each.

"Okay," he said. "Let's go."

First they had to get away from the humans.

And the sheep.

Limpy didn't particularly want to run into the rude ants again either.

The three of them hurried along the platform, keeping to the shadows and watching anxiously for boots.

Then Charm let out a terrified croak.

"Look out!"

Limpy turned.

A large gate was swinging open and a truck was backing through it, heading straight toward them. Limpy had never seen a truck drive backward before. It was a chilling sight.

Stack me, thought Limpy. This must be how trucks sneak up on cane toads when they're not expecting it.

"Low mongrels!" yelled Goliath. He looked around for a weapon, saw a big rusty nail poking out of a rotting fence post, dragged it out, and waved it angrily at the truck. "Let's see how you like it when I slash your tires and scratch your paint and stab your fuel tank and drink all your gasoline!"

Limpy and Charm grabbed the loose skin under Goliath's arms and struggled to hold him back.

"Dunno why I'm doing this," muttered Charm. "A few truck wheels over his head would do him good."

Limpy looked around desperately for a way to escape.

They were trapped between the truck and the fence and the steep edge of the platform.

Then Limpy saw a weed-covered plastic grate in the concrete near their feet. It was covering a hole.

"Quick, Goliath," he said. "Help me get this open."

Limpy grabbed the grate and started pulling at it. Charm helped him. The truck was getting closer. Goliath gave it a last scowl as he hooked his nail under the rim of the grate and prized it up. Together, panting, they rolled the grate away from the hole.

Charm looked nervously down into the darkness.

"Do all wombat holes in towns have lids?" she said.

"It's a drain," said Limpy. "Like the stormwater one under our highway at home. Jump!"

The truck was almost on top of them. Limpy

decided this wasn't the time to tell Charm about what humans use sewers for.

He pushed Charm into the hole. Goliath squeezed in after her. Limpy followed. As he fell, he closed his eyes and thought of their lovely swamp. He wished he could land with a squish into soft, familiar mud.

Instead, he landed with a painful thud and a splash.

"You okay?" said Goliath's voice in the gloom. "I'm okay, and I think Charm's okay 'cause she's biting my knee."

Limpy checked to make sure that he could move all his limbs and warts.

"I'm okay," he said.

Above them, one of the truck wheels rolled over the hole and stopped, blocking out the circle of daylight.

They were in total darkness.

"I don't like towns," said Charm in a small voice.

Limpy reached out till he felt her arm and gave it a gentle squeeze.

"Don't worry," he said. "We'll be in the national park soon."

He heard his voice echo down what sounded like a tunnel. He was surprised to hear how confident it sounded, because he didn't feel very confident at all.

"Which way do we go?" asked Goliath.

Limpy could feel water trickling over his feet.

83

Fortunately, it didn't seem to have lumps in it.

"This water must be going somewhere," he said. "Let's follow it."

They set off, hopping slowly and cautiously.

Limpy reached out in the darkness for Charm's hand.

Poor kid, he thought. She didn't ask to be here.

He gave her hand a squeeze.

"Thanks," said Goliath. "That feels good."

"Limpy," said Charm. "Do you actually know where the national park is?"

Limpy let go of Goliath's hand and hesitated before he answered.

If I was Malcolm, he said to himself, I'd say "Yes, of course. I know exactly where it is. Follow me." But I'm not, I'm Limpy.

He took a deep breath.

"Yes," he said. "Of course. I know exactly where it is. Follow me."

"Where?" said Goliath.

Limpy thought about confessing that he didn't know exactly where it was at all. Then he remembered the adoring way Charm had looked at Malcolm. And how jealous he'd felt.

"To the east," said Limpy.

They hopped along the tunnel in darkness and silence.

Crunch.

Limpy stiffened.

What was that sound?

Slurp.

He relaxed. It was just Goliath eating something.

"Mmm," said Goliath. "The flying beetles in here are delicious."

"Actually," said an annoyed voice, "we're cockroaches."

"Sorry," said Goliath. "My mistake."

Crunch.

Slurp.

After a while the blackness up ahead started fuzzing into gray. As they moved toward it, the gray got lighter and a white circle slowly came into focus.

"The end of the tunnel," said Limpy.

He saw that Charm was peering anxiously ahead, her dear little face straining to see what they were moving toward.

Limpy peered as well.

The light was too bright to see anything clearly, and his eyes were still getting used to it when in front of him suddenly loomed three big dark shapes.

"Hmmm," said a voice. "Here's something a bit more interesting than cockroaches."

The voice was deep and soft and menacing.

Limpy pulled Charm close to him and froze.

A big round furry whiskered face was blocking their way, with two others behind it.

Cats.

"Hungry?" purred the front cat, a ginger one with a smug smile, to the other two, one white and one gray.

"Starving," said Goliath. "Cockroaches just don't fill you up. Eat a swarm and two hops later you're still hungry. . . ."

His voice trailed off.

Limpy's throat sac was aching with fright.

The cats yawned. Their teeth looked very sharp. They lazily stretched their claws. Which looked even sharper.

"Just before you start ripping us to pieces," said Limpy, struggling to stop his voice from wobbling, "I would like to point out we have glands full of poison."

"And," said Charm, "they're aimed right at you."

"And," said Goliath, "I'm very good at arm wrestling."

The ginger cat smirked. "Poison, eh? That's a good one."

Limpy's insides sagged.

"Let's squirt 'em," muttered Goliath.

Limpy felt the same way, but there was a problem. With Charm's poison sacs being so small, they might not have enough pus between them to deal with three fully grown cats.

Oh well, thought Limpy. We'll soon know.

Then Limpy heard the white cat, who was looking concerned, whisper to the ginger one, "Cane toads."

The ginger cat's face dropped. It looked at Limpy more closely.

"Ah," it said.

The cats glanced at one another, then took a step back.

"Here's what we should probably do," said the ginger cat to Limpy. "We should probably agree that we won't rip you to shreds if you don't squirt poison in our eyes."

Limpy nodded gratefully.

"It's a deal," whispered Charm.

"No it's not," said Goliath.

Limpy stared at him, horrified.

"There's something else we want as well," said Goliath to the cats. "We want to know where the national park is."

The ginger cat looked at Goliath, then grinned.

"You want to go to the national park?" it said.

"Yeah," said Goliath.

"Yes, please," said Limpy.

The cats grinned at one another. Then the ginger one turned and pointed.

"There it is."

Limpy was so surprised and excited, he forgot to be

scared of the cats. He hopped past them and out of the tunnel.

At last.

He'd found it.

The national park he'd dreamed about so often.

Limpy's eyes were used to the light now, and he could see exactly what was spread out in front of him.

His face fell.

"This is it?" he croaked. "This is the national park?"

"Yes," sniggered the cats behind him.

Limpy stared.

In front of him, stretching in a rippling sweep all the way to the horizon, was nothing but water.

15

Limpy had never seen so much water.

Not even the time it rained nonstop for ages and the water in the swamp rose so quickly that Limpy had to drag the flat rellies to higher ground and Goliath found his lunch (bog weevils and mud leeches) hiding up a tree.

This was a million times more water.

"It's flooded," said Limpy, dizzy with disappointment. "The national park's flooded."

He turned to ask the cats how long it had been like this, but they'd vanished.

"It can't all be flooded," said Charm. "There must be some high ground that's not flooded."

Limpy thought about this. She was probably right. A national park would have to have high bits. For the rock wallabies and the goats and the kookaburras who wanted to laugh at one another over long distances.

"I can't see any high bits," said Goliath.

Limpy pointed to where the water met the sky. "They're probably so far away we can't see them from here."

"Too far to swim," said Charm.

"And cane toads can't fly," said Goliath gloomily. "Not unless Mum and Dad have been hiding something."

Limpy sighed. Just hearing the names Mum and Dad made him feel sad.

"Pity we can't swim as fast as that animal," said Goliath.

Limpy peered over to where Goliath was pointing. A familiar object was speeding through the water. Limpy had often seen ones like it being towed on trailers behind cars.

"It's not an animal," said Limpy. "It's a boat."

"Whatever," said Goliath gloomily. "Pity we haven't got one of those frothy things hanging off our bottoms to make us whiz through the water."

Limpy stared at the outboard motor at the back of the boat.

An idea hit him.

"Good thinking, Goliath," he murmured.

His thoughts were shattered by a scream.

A human scream.

Limpy looked around, heart in his throat sac.

Four nearly naked humans were standing under a palm tree, pointing at him and Charm and Goliath and yelling.

Stack me, thought Limpy, grabbing Charm and Goliath protectively. Where did they come from? Then he realized why he hadn't seen them before. Their sunburned skin was the same color as their parrot-red picnic blanket.

Camouflage.

"Hop for it," he said to Charm and Goliath. "I'll distract them."

The two kid humans were advancing across the sand, waving plastic spades menacingly. The mum and dad humans were right behind them, waving metal barbecue tongs even more menacingly.

"No offense, Limpy," said Charm, "but hopping in circles isn't going to fool them for long. I think it's better if Goliath distracts them."

"I agree," said Goliath.

Before Limpy could stop him, Goliath hopped toward the humans, yelling, "Hey, you overcooked land worms! Get your big bums over here! Catch me if you can!"

Limpy decided to get Charm to safety, then go and help Goliath.

That was his plan, right up until he saw the cooler lid lying on the picnic blanket.

"Look," said Limpy, warts tingling with excitement. "Our boat."

Charm frowned.

"Don't boats need outboard motors?" she said.

"Don't worry," said Limpy. "I've got a plan."

As soon as he and Charm had dragged the cooler lid into a thick patch of undergrowth, Limpy peered anxiously across the sand to see how Goliath was doing.

He couldn't see Goliath anywhere.

Neither could the humans. They were wandering around on the sand, swinging their weapons in puzzled frustration.

Goliath had vanished.

"Where is he?" asked Charm anxiously.

"He'll be okay," said Limpy. "He's been dodging trucks since he first got legs. Goliath'll be fine."

Limpy wished he felt as confident as he sounded.

He and Charm crouched in the undergrowth and watched the humans hunting for Goliath. When the humans couldn't find him, they started hunting for their cooler lid. When they couldn't find that, they packed up the rest of their stuff and stamped away, grumbling.

Limpy and Charm crept out of their hiding place.

"Goliath," they called. "Where are you?"

No reply.

Oh no, thought Limpy. Perhaps Goliath's run into the cats again.

He had a horrible vision involving a cat and Goliath and dinner.

Limpy shuddered.

It was too awful to think about.

If Goliath tried to eat a cat, he'd choke.

"Goliath!" yelled Limpy desperately. "Where are you?"

"Here," croaked a gravelly voice behind them.

Limpy spun round.

Goliath was standing there, spitting out sand. He had sand on his head and sand on his warts and sand in the folds of his skin.

"Where have you been?" gasped Charm.

"Doing something I learned from Limpy," croaked Goliath. "He copied an echidna with that Uncle Nick idea. Well, I've been copying our friends the sand-worms. Burrowed myself into the sand. I was able to thank them for the idea, 'cause I met quite a few while I was down there. Very tasty, but a bit gritty."

Limpy gently brushed the sand off Goliath's warts. "Thanks, Goliath," he said. "You saved us."

"That was a really brave thing to do," said Charm. "When Malcolm hears about it, he'll be really impressed."

Goliath screwed up his face, and for a second

Limpy thought he was going to explode. But all he said was, "Ouch. Sand in my eyes. I need mucus."

Limpy and Charm hastily spat mucus into Goliath's eyes.

"That's better," breathed Goliath. "Thanks."

Then he saw the cooler lid.

"What's that?" he asked.

"Our boat," replied Limpy.

"Doesn't a boat need one of those frothy things at the back?" said Goliath.

"Don't worry," said Limpy. "I've got a plan." He pointed to a nearby clump of stinkweed. "Start eating."

The launching of the boat was a big success.

Limpy and Charm and Goliath dragged it down to the water and pushed it in.

"It floats!" shouted Charm.

They loaded it with stinkweed and other supplies and clambered aboard.

"It still floats," shouted Goliath, but not as loud as Charm because his tummy was so full of stinkweed.

"Okay," said Limpy. "Outboard motor in position, please."

Goliath hung on to the back of the cooler lid and lowered his bottom into the water.

Soon bubbles appeared behind him; then the water frothed and the cooler lid lurched forward.

"Hooray!" shouted Charm. "We're off. National park, here we come."

As they chugged out into the open water, Limpy turned and faced the horizon, enjoying the fresh breeze on his face.

Somewhere out there was the place where Mum and Dad and the others could live safely forever. And he was closer to it than he'd ever been.

For the first time in quite a while, Limpy felt a glow of happiness.

"How long will it take us to get there?" asked Charm.

"Not long," said Limpy. "Not long."

Limpy tried to work out how long they'd been drifting.

Hours?

Days?

The stinkweed had run out just before dark, and Goliath's bottom bubbles soon after. Then there'd been a night, and a sunrise, and lots and lots of hot sun.

The answer, thought Limpy weakly, is ages.

"This is the longest boat trip I've ever been on," croaked Goliath.

Limpy didn't bother to point out it was the only boat trip Goliath had ever been on. Like Goliath, he was so weak with thirst and hunger he could hardly speak. He was exhausted just lying next to Charm and Goliath on the cooler lid. Even groaning was too much effort.

"I wish we could drink the water," croaked Charm.

Limpy gave her hand a sympathetic squeeze.

He wished they could too. That had been the biggest disappointment of the whole trip. Gulping a mouthful of the water they were floating on and discovering it tasted like the salt-and-vinegar chips humans threw out of cars, only without the vinegar.

"Untidy mongrels," croaked Goliath. "They must have chucked millions of chips in the water to make it this salty."

Charm and Limpy croaked their agreement.

With a big effort Limpy managed to lift the palm frond off his head and squint at the horizon.

Still nothing.

No national park hills.

No treetops.

No rocky outcrops.

No kookaburras standing on one another's shoulders.

Just flat water and the empty blue sky and the scorching, scorching sun.

Limpy let the palm frond drop back onto his head.

Without these to give us some shade, he thought feebly but gratefully, we'd be dryer and stiffer than poor Uncle Nick by now.

He felt a surge of gratitude to Charm for suggesting they bring the palm fronds in the first place. And a surge of relief that Goliath hadn't been able to eat them when he'd tried to earlier in the day.

Goliath's pleading voice brought Limpy back to the painful present.

"Food," croaked Goliath from under his palm frond. "I need food."

"There's only a tiny bit left," said Charm.

"That'll do," said Goliath. "I'll have that."

Limpy raised his frond and reminded Goliath that they'd agreed to ration out the food so it would last them the trip.

"Just give me some of it," begged Goliath.

"All we've got," said Charm, "is three flying-beetle legs and a sandworm snout."

"Anything," croaked Goliath. "Please. I'm a growing toad. I need food."

"Hang on a sec," said Charm, peering into the leaf she'd wrapped the food in. "Someone's eaten the snout and replaced it with a bit of dried mucus."

Limpy looked at Goliath.

Goliath went guiltily silent.

"All right," he said after a while. "I'll just have the mucus."

Charm gave Goliath two beetle legs. His eyes opened wide with delight. She handed the other one to Limpy.

"What about you?" said Limpy. Goliath was already crunching the two legs and sucking the juice gratefully. Limpy held the third leg out to Charm. "You have it."

"It's okay," said Charm. "I don't need much food. That's the one advantage of being stunted by pollution as a kid. Tiny tummy."

Tiny tummy, thought Limpy emotionally as he crunched his beetle leg, but very big heart.

Limpy lay on the cooler lid and lost track of time again.

Then he felt Charm slip under his palm frond and put her arms round him.

"Limpy," she said in a tiny exhausted voice. "We're not going to find the national park, are we? We're just going to keep on drifting till we dry out and die."

Limpy couldn't answer her, partly because his mucus was almost solid and partly because he had a terrible aching fear she was right.

He hugged her tight.

"I don't mind dying," she said. "It was worth it, trying to find the national park. I'm just sad I won't ever see Malcolm again."

Limpy was glad he couldn't speak. He might say something about Malcolm that would upset Charm, and he didn't want to do that.

"I know he's not perfect," continued Charm. "But I think he likes me, and that makes me feel really good. Because he's so big and handsome and I'm so small and ugly."

A spasm of love ran through Limpy's chest, and it made sad dribbles of mucus run out of his eyes. He licked them up and swallowed them to make his voice work.

"Charm," he croaked. "You're not ugly. You're . . ."

Before Limpy could tell her she was beautiful, plus the best sister in the whole universe and the nicest individual he'd ever met, he was interrupted by a scream from Goliath.

"Look!" Goliath yelled. "Food! Heaps of it!"

Limpy scrambled out from under the frond.

Goliath was on his feet, jumping up and down excitedly, pointing at the water.

"Look!" he shouted. "Peeled slime grubs stuffed with mashed ants. Fresh locust breast accompanied by mosquito-and-centipede salad. Snail guts on the half shell."

Limpy hung on to the edge of the wildly rocking cooler lid and stared at where Goliath was pointing.

All he could see was water.

"I'll get it!" yelled Goliath.

Limpy realized his cousin was going to dive in.

"Grab him!" said Charm.

They grabbed Goliath's skin folds and dragged him down onto the lid.

"Locust breast," sobbed Goliath. "I saw it."

"He's delirious," said Charm. "Seeing things.

Dehydration can do that. I saw a drought-affected galah once who thought Goliath was a tree stump."

"Snail guts," moaned Goliath.

Limpy glanced at the patch of water Goliath had been pointing at, just in case. And saw, below the surface, a dark shape.

He looked more closely. The shape was too big to be any of the food items Goliath had mentioned. Even a jumbo slime grub wasn't anything like that big. What it looked like, Limpy realized, warts tingling, was the smooth top of a small hill.

A small hill in a national park.

"Yes!" screamed Limpy, suddenly bursting with more energy than he'd had all day. "We've found it. It's not much, but it's a start."

The small hilltop broke through the surface of the water.

Limpy's excitement evaporated.

Two eyes were looking at him from under what Limpy now realized wasn't a hilltop. Two eyes in a creased and warty face.

"Stack me," croaked Goliath. "It's a giant cane toad."

Limpy stared. Was it possible? Had a cane toad made the journey before them to find the national park?

"Cripes," said Goliath. "It's bigger than Malcolm."

Limpy looked more closely. The curved brown

thing he'd mistaken for a hilltop was attached to the toad's back. Was it a cooler lid that had melted in the sun?

"Excuse me," said Limpy. "Are you a cane toad?"

The face looked offended.

"Certainly not," it said. "I'm a giant turtle."

"Sorry," said Limpy. "Um, you don't happen to know if there are any higher-up bits of the national park around here, do you? Bits that haven't been flooded?"

The turtle frowned. "Flooded?" it said. "None of the national park's been flooded. It's always like this. This is the ocean."

Limpy didn't understand. But he could feel something gnawing at his guts that wasn't hunger.

"What do you mean?" he asked.

"The Great Barrier Reef national park," said the turtle. "It's down there, under the water. You're floating on it."

Limpy leaned over the side of the cooler lid, stuck his head in the water, and looked around.

The salt burned his eyes and made everything faint and blurry.

But he could still see enough.

Hills and valleys and long wavy grass, and creatures that Limpy was pretty sure were going about their business safely and securely.

He felt himself slipping off the cooler lid. He pulled his head out of the water and regained his balance.

"We've found it," he said excitedly. "The national park."

"Limpy," said Charm. "It's underwater. We can't live underwater. We need air."

"And flying insects," said Goliath, peering hopefully at a speck of dirt on the cooler lid. "Poop, I thought that was a gnat."

Limpy sighed. He loved his sister and cousin heaps, but sometimes they could be a bit thick.

"I know we need air," said Limpy. "But don't forget we can breathe through our skin. We just need to make sure a bit of our skin's above the water."

Charm and Goliath looked doubtful.

"Excuse me," said the turtle. "This is a very interesting conversation, but I've only got another three hundred years to live and I've got things to do. Goodbye."

The turtle dived down into the depths.

"Look," said Limpy, pointing to the disappearing turtle. "His feet are webbed, like ours. I reckon we can learn to live in water too."

Charm rolled her eyes.

"What about that time you came down the mud slide too fast and nearly drowned in the swamp?" she said.

"I was young and careless," said Limpy. "I forgot to leave part of me sticking out of the water. This time I've got a plan. I'll hang over the side of the cooler lid and you hold on to my feet. That way I can breathe through my bottom."

Slowly Limpy's eyes got used to the salt water.

Wow, he thought.

He'd never seen so much food.

The water was full of it.

Fish and yabbies and worms and slugs and heaps of other delicious-looking food items, all swarming and darting and slithering around.

This is perfect, thought Limpy.

And everything was so colorful.

"Wow," he said out loud, making bubbles. His mouth filled up with salty water, which wasn't quite so perfect, but he didn't care.

This was heaven.

He wondered if nature had made all this food different colors for a reason. Perhaps to help consumers make a choice. Blue for breakfast, yellow for lunch, purple for tea, that sort of thing.

The food at home was mostly brown or gray. It was so boring to look at that sometimes Goliath turned a lizard inside out before he ate it, just to make it a bit more colorful.

We wouldn't have to do that with this tucker, thought Limpy happily.

There was only one problem.

With Charm and Goliath holding on to his legs above the surface, he couldn't reach any of it.

"Deeper?" said Charm as Limpy clambered back onto the cooler lid. Her little face furrowed with concern. "If you go any deeper, you'll drown."

"Not," said Limpy, "if I have something to breathe through."

He looked around the cooler lid and saw just the thing.

The sun had dried the palm fronds to a crisp. He grabbed one and stripped off the shriveled leaves.

"This'll do it," he said. He stuck one end of the long fat hollow stem into his mouth. "You both hang on to the other end and don't let it go under the surface, okay?"

Charm and Goliath looked at him, puzzled.

Limpy took the stem out of his mouth and said it again.

Understanding dawned on their faces. "Oh, right," said Goliath. "I thought you said you wanted us both to jump in with you."

Limpy slid down through the sunlit depths until he was standing on a colorful rocky outcrop shaped like a pile of wombat intestines. Fields of pastel ferns rippled slowly in the warm currents, delicate as the most delicate ribbons of mucus. Next to Limpy was a cliff face covered in beautiful patterns of little bumps, like the inside of a lizard's stomach.

This is almost as beautiful as the swamp at home, thought Limpy. If it had some mud, it would be.

He sucked in a lungful of air through the palm stem and blew out a cascade of sparkling bubbles.

Nearby, a blue and pink and silver yabbie strolled along a row of tiny trees that seemed to be made of mouse brains.

Limpy waved.

The yabbie waved back.

What a wonderful place to live, thought Limpy happily.

He smiled as he imagined Mum and Dad's faces when they saw it. Mum had always particularly liked the look of mouse brains.

Then he felt a stab in his guts as he remembered the virus germs. Which meant he wouldn't actually be able to see Mum and Dad in their new home.

Ever.

It was too upsetting to think about, so Limpy concentrated on the other pangs in his guts. The hunger ones.

No wonder I'm so hungry, he thought. I've only eaten one beetle leg all day.

Limpy hopped down to the next rock ledge and picked up a delicious-looking green and black and orange slug.

"I'm very salty," said the slug. "You probably won't like me."

Limpy gave the slug a smile for trying to be helpful. He wasn't worried. His eyes had got used to the salt, so he was pretty sure his tummy could.

Limpy sucked another lungful of air through the stem.

Only this time it wasn't air, it was water.

Choking and spluttering and panicking, Limpy realized what must have happened. When he hopped down lower, he must have pulled the top of the stem under the water.

"Palm stem snorkles only work if you keep one end out of the water," said the slug.

Limpy put the slug back on the rock ledge. He didn't smile at it this time. He was too busy wondering why Goliath and Charm hadn't held on to the stem and stopped him from dragging it under.

Air bubbles, thought Limpy desperately. I need air bubbles.

He looked around, hoping to see some of his old ones hanging around. If he could get them back inside him, they might relieve the pain that was starting in his lungs.

He couldn't see a single bubble.

Just Goliath and Charm, a palm stem in each of their mouths, floating nearby and smiling and waving.

They'd jumped in too.

"No!" said Limpy in despair.

His last air bubble wobbled out of his mouth and drifted away.

Why couldn't they have waited till I got back on the cooler lid? he thought bitterly. I'd have given them a turn.

His lungs were burning. Even as he signaled to Charm and Goliath that he was heading to the surface, he saw Goliath lunge at a blue and yellow fish and then start choking and spluttering in a cloud of bubbles. Goliath's stem must have filled with water too.

Come on, Limpy begged them silently. Follow me.

He kicked his feet and headed for the surface.

As he rose through the water, lungs on fire, a horrible thought hit him. If all three of them were down here, nobody was looking after the cooler lid.

What if it had floated away?

He peered up, trying to see it.

There it was. A dark rectangular shape up above.

That's a relief, thought Limpy.

He didn't actually feel much relief, because his chest was hurting too much.

He felt a bit of anxiety, though, when he got closer to the surface and saw that the dark shape was very big to be a cooler lid.

Too big.

And he definitely felt the huge jolt of fear that

stabbed through him when he spotted a movement out of the corner of his eye and turned and saw what was swimming toward him.

It was pink and brown, with blue webbed feet and dark humps on its back and a plastic pipe in its mouth that distorted its face into a leer of hatred.

A human.

18

Limpy swam for his life.

He didn't get far. His legs were frozen with fear, and his arms weren't working properly either.

Must be because I've run out of air, Limpy thought helplessly, his lungs screaming.

The human glided toward him through the shadowy water, eyes big and scary behind a face mask.

Limpy kept as still as he could, hoping the human would think he was a larger-than-usual speck of plankton.

At least I can't see any weapons, thought Limpy. No tennis racquets, no golf clubs, no folding chairs. Though a whack round the head from those metal tanks on the human's back could be lethal.

The human swam right up to Limpy so their faces were almost touching.

Limpy smiled weakly. It was important to look the

part. Plankton were probably pretty happy, even the larger-than-usual ones.

The human stared at him.

Limpy could see a frown behind the face mask.

This is a national park, Limpy reminded the human silently. You're not allowed to kill me here.

The human kept on staring.

Limpy would have held his breath if he'd had any to hold.

Then a shoal of brightly colored food items swam close to the human's head and the human, with a final puzzled glance at Limpy, swam away after them.

Limpy, chest almost bursting, struggled to the surface.

"Yes!" he screamed as his head burst into sunlight and he sucked sweet air in through his mouth and every pore in his face.

The human hadn't killed him.

The national park was everything he'd hoped for.

Okay, except for the water.

Charm and Goliath's gasping heads appeared next to him.

Limpy turned to tell them that things were looking fairly good, but as he did, he saw that things weren't looking good at all.

The water around them was full of humans swimming facedown and breathing through plastic tubes.

"Stack me!" spluttered Goliath. "The mongrels have stolen our idea."

Limpy was glad they had. With their faces in the water, the humans hadn't seen him and Charm and Goliath yet. But they could at any moment. And what if the surface of the water wasn't part of the national park? What if, when the humans took their face masks off and saw three cane toads treading water, they reached for their golf clubs before you could say "Cane toad hunting season is open"?

Limpy looked desperately around for the cooler lid.

It was gone.

Instead, looming over them was a gleaming white boat, bigger than any Limpy had seen on the highway. More humans with face masks were clambering down ladders fixed to the side of the boat and lowering themselves into the water.

"We've got to hide," said Limpy.

"Where?" said Charm. "The palm fronds have gone, and we can't go back under the water because we haven't got tubes."

Goliath scowled. "I could bash some humans and grab some," he said.

Limpy sighed.

"The whole point of hiding," he said, "is so the humans don't notice us. I think they probably will if you start bashing them."

"Not if I do it gently," said Goliath.

Charm grabbed Limpy's arm.

"There's only one place we can hide," she said.

Limpy knew she was right. The idea terrified him. But it was their only choice, and they had to do it fast.

The hardest part was climbing up the big slippery chain.

Luckily, it was hanging off the other side of the boat from where most of the humans were swimming, but Limpy was still scared.

He knew a boat chain definitely wasn't part of a national park. If he and Charm and Goliath were spotted, the humans could bash them with any type of sporting equipment quite legally.

Limpy didn't say anything to the others. But when they finally clambered through a hole in the top of the boat and flopped down gratefully onto a cool metal floor, he trembled with relief.

"Good on you Limpy," said Charm. "I was worried about you, climbing that slippery chain with your leg."

"Thanks," said Limpy.

"It wasn't easy for me either," said Goliath. "I'm

weak with hunger, plus I've got a splinter in my toe."

"I was worried about you too, Goliath," said Charm.

"Thanks," said Goliath. "I've got a slight headache as well."

Limpy looked around. They were in a big area full of machinery that he guessed was for making the boat go, or grinding up cane toads, or possibly both.

There were no humans around.

"We'll be safe here for a while," said Limpy. "As long as we keep our heads down. Give us a chance to think about how we can find another national park."

"One that's not underwater," said Charm.

"No," said Goliath. "I can't do it. I can't go looking for another national park. Not without food. I need food. There must be a picnic area on this boat. Or a worm farm."

Goliath was already hopping toward an open doorway.

"Don't be stupid," said Charm, hurrying after him. "Come back."

Limpy hurried after them both. This was what he'd dreaded. Nothing could stop Goliath when he was hungry.

Except possibly a human with a large meat hammer.

As Limpy clambered over the metal wall at the bottom of the doorway, he saw that Goliath was already halfway along the passage on the other side.

"Goliath!" yelled Limpy. "If Ancient Eric were here, he'd be telling you to come back immediately."

Limpy knew that wasn't strictly true. If poor Ancient Eric were there, a human would probably be using him as a floatie, but it was worth a try.

Goliath didn't even slow down.

Limpy went after him.

Hopping in circles wasn't a problem in the passageway. Limpy just bounced from wall to wall and made good progress. Right up until he reached Charm, who was standing frozen, staring into a room off one side of the passage.

Limpy saw that his sister was trembling with shock.

"What's the matter?" he asked, putting his arm round her.

She didn't reply.

Limpy peered into the room and saw it was a sort of shop, with racks of postcards and a big glass cupboard full of soft drinks.

Even though Charm's little body was white with salt and Limpy knew she must be as thirsty as he was, she wasn't looking at the soft drinks.

She was looking up at the shelves.

The shelves were piled with the sorts of things humans bought when they were on holiday. Sunglasses and plastic boats and pens with plankton in them. The sort of stuff that broke easily and got chucked out of cars on the way home.

Limpy realized Charm wasn't trembling because of the flimsiness of human souvenirs.

She was trembling because of the cane toads squatting on the middle shelf.

Limpy felt a shiver go down his back.

For a fleeting second he thought they were alive.

Then he realized they weren't. They were too shiny and still, and their eyes were too glassy. And they were doing something no live cane toad would ever do. They were holding miniature items of human sporting equipment.

Tennis racquets.

Cricket bats.

Golf clubs.

That's disgusting, thought Limpy. Making them pose with the very weapons that probably killed them.

Charm gave a small sob.

Limpy's heart ached. He wished she didn't have to see this. He wished he could take her home, where at least dead cane toads had flatness and dignity.

Then he remembered the virus germs. Was poor Charm imagining herself with the other cane toads on the shelf?

"Come on," said Limpy softly, steering her away from the shop. "We can't do anything for them now. It's more important that we find Goliath."

At that moment, from along the passage, came a loud burp.

Goliath had found food.

Goliath was in another room further along the passage.

"Look," he said, chewing happily. "Isn't this great?"

Limpy froze.

The room was full of humans. They were standing against the walls on all sides. Goliath hadn't even seen them.

Limpy dived in front of Charm and braced himself for an attack.

It didn't come.

Weak with relief, Limpy saw why. The things towering over him weren't humans after all. Just human clothes hanging on pegs.

Goliath was chewing a sock.

"Help yourself," he said, pointing to the bags and rucksacks on the floor.

Limpy saw that Goliath had opened several rucksacks and emptied out the contents. He was sitting among cosmetic bags and books and maps and underwear.

"There's plenty for everyone," said Goliath. "I recommend those delicious deodorant sticks that humans rub under their arms."

Limpy remembered how hungry he was.

He started checking the hairbrushes for head lice. Then he saw something that drove all thoughts of food from his mind and tummy.

Spilling out of one rucksack were some photos of humans standing under trees. The trees were full of brightly colored birds. Some of the humans had birds standing on their heads and shoulders.

Limpy peered more closely.

One of the humans was holding a frog.

The humans looked happy.

The birds looked happy.

The frog looked happy.

Limpy's warts tingled with excitement. This was exactly how he'd imagined a national park would be. No birds being shot. No frogs being dissected by scientists. Limpy studied the photos for any signs of cane toads being bashed or run over.

Not a single one.

And everything was surrounded by air, not water.

This must be another national park, thought Limpy. It's got to be.

He was about to show the photos to Charm and Goliath when he saw something else on the floor. Something that made his warts almost pop with happiness.

A pair of human shoes, caked with mud.

"Look," croaked Limpy. "Mud."

"Thanks," said Goliath with his mouth full. "But I prefer sock fluff."

"Don't you see?" said Limpy. "The underwater national park isn't the only one these humans have visited. They've also been to one with mud. They could be going to others. They could be visiting another mud national park tomorrow."

Charm and Goliath stared at him.

"We could go with them," said Limpy.

A half-chewed hairbrush fell from Goliath's mouth.

"You mean risk being bashed by a mob of humans just to see if they're going to another national park?" said Charm.

"This is our last chance to find a safe place for Mum and Dad and the others," said Limpy. "What have we got to lose? If we give up now, none of us are going to survive."

Charm nodded slowly.

Limpy was glad he hadn't needed to use the words "virus germs."

"Let me get this right," said Goliath, frowning. "You want us to hide in these rucksacks and not eat too noisily?"

"No," said Limpy. "That's too risky. If the humans find us, they'll kill us before we even arrive at the national park."

"So," said Charm, frowning too. "How are we going to get them to take us?"

Limpy squatted on the shelf and held the little tennis racquet over his head.

"The vital thing," he whispered to Charm and Goliath, who were squatting next to him, "is not to move."

"This soft drink tickles," complained Goliath.

Limpy knew what he meant. But it looked good. As it dried on their skin, it was starting to shine just like the varnish on the poor stuffed cane toads behind them on the shelf.

"Charm," whispered Limpy. "Hold your golf club a bit higher."

Charm did.

"Goliath," said Limpy. "Try not to look as though you want to hit a human with that cricket bat."

"But I do," said Goliath.

Limpy sighed.

In the distance he could hear the humans clambering back onto the boat after their swim.

"What will we do," whispered Charm, "if they don't want to buy any souvenirs?"

"If they don't want to buy me," said Goliath, "I'll squirt them."

Limpy tried to sigh again and found that the soft drink had stuck his lips together.

The humans wanted to buy lots of things.

They crowded into the shop, jostling and chattering in their weird human language.

Limpy wished he could understand what they were saying.

What he hoped they were saying was, "We'll take the three cane toads at the front. Please wrap them up really gently, and do it quickly because we're leaving now for another national park."

What he feared they were saying was, "We're so thirsty after swimming in that salty chip water, we don't give a flying bog weevil about souvenirs; all we want are drinks."

Limpy felt something tickling his foot. He looked down. A little spider was brushing past his toes. With tiny movements himself, ones he hoped were invisible, Limpy licked his lips till he could move them.

"G'day," whispered Limpy to the spider. "Can you

understand what the humans are saying?"

The spider stared at Limpy in shock.

"Yikes!" it said. "A battery-operated cane toad. Now I've seen everything."

At that moment a human reached over and picked Limpy up.

Don't move, Limpy told himself. Whatever you do, don't move.

It was fairly easy not to at first because he was rigid with fear. But then the human shifted her fingers to the ticklish spot on Limpy's tummy, and suddenly he was struggling not to giggle.

The adult human held him up in front of a child human.

Limpy stared pleadingly at the human boy's friendly freckled face.

Please don't notice I'm alive, he begged silently.

"Look," said the mother, "isn't he cute?"

Limpy hoped she'd said, "Look, isn't he dead?"

The human boy stared sadly at Limpy.

"That's really cruel," he said. "Killing them just to make souvenirs. I'd only want a cane toad if I could have a live one for a pet."

Limpy hoped he'd said, "That's a lovely souvenir, Mummy, but it makes me a bit sad only having one. Can I have three?"

The mother obviously couldn't afford three, because

she put Limpy back on the shelf. Limpy saw the spider nearby, watching with interest.

"Why didn't they want me?" whispered Limpy.

"'Cause you're dead," said the spider.

While Limpy was trying to make sense of this, another human picked Goliath up.

"Boy," said the human, putting his red face close to Goliath's. "This one's ugly."

Limpy knew the human had said something not very nice from the expression on the human's face. Limpy looked anxiously at Goliath, whose eyes, he saw, were bulging in a worrying way.

Don't spray him, Goliath, begged Limpy silently. Please don't.

Then yet another human picked Limpy up and held him out to the woman who was collecting the money.

They said lots of things to each other. The man prodded Limpy quite a bit and turned him upside down a couple of times. Finally, sick and giddy, Limpy found himself lying on a paper bag. Goliath, he saw, was being put into another bag.

The spider was nearby.

"He's bought you," said the spider. "And his mate's bought the big ugly one next to you. Yours got the best deal, though. A dollar off, 'cause of your crook leg."

125

Limpy's stomach lurched as he felt himself being picked up again.

He peered desperately around the shop, and just before he was dropped into the bag, he saw the thing he had feared the most.

His stomach went beyond lurching, into stabs of anguish.

Charm, her tiny face frozen in an expression of hope and anxiety, was still on the shelf.

21

Limpy had never been a souvenir before.

It wasn't very comfortable.

It's this paper bag, he said to himself in the darkness. It's just too small for a cane toad and a plastic yabbie and a plankton pen with a really sharp point.

Limpy wished the human who'd bought him yesterday had taken him out of the bag before putting him in the rucksack. Even though that would have meant the human touching him again.

Limpy shivered at the memory.

The rucksack jolted. Limpy was stabbed in the bottom again, either by the pen or the yabbie, or possibly both.

When he'd managed to wriggle away from them a bit, he wondered how Goliath was doing.

"Goliath," called Limpy softly. "These paper bags are a real pain, eh?"

"Not really," said Goliath's voice from the next rucksack. "I've eaten half of mine."

Limpy smiled.

Good old Goliath. He could make you smile even when your bottom was hurting and your back was itching and you were covered with human fingerprints and you were worried sick about Charm.

For the millionth time, Limpy hoped that Charm had been bought as well. If possible, by friends of his human, which would mean she'd be in a rucksack not too far away from the one he was in.

"Charm," he called for the millionth time. "Are you okay?"

No reply.

Perhaps she can't hear me over the noise of the bus engine, thought Limpy.

He was pretty sure it was a bus engine.

The boat-rocking had stopped soon after Limpy was first put in the rucksack. Then there'd been a bit of jiggling that felt like the rucksack was on a human's back. Then no movement during what Limpy assumed was the night. Now Limpy was pretty sure this jolting was a bus.

"Goliath," called Limpy. "Have you heard from Charm yet?"

"No," said Goliath's voice. "Why, doesn't she want her paper bag?"

Limpy wished he were more like Goliath.

If I had a smaller brain and a bigger stomach, he thought, perhaps I wouldn't worry so much.

About Charm.

About the virus germs,

About whether the bus really was heading to another national park.

About what would happen if they couldn't escape from their humans and had to spend the rest of their lives on a mantelpiece.

What I need, thought Limpy, is something to take my mind off things.

He started eating his paper bag.

The bus stopped with a jolt.

Limpy winced, pulled the plankton pen out of his bottom, and listened.

The humans were getting off the bus.

This was the moment Limpy had been waiting for. "We're at the national park and Charm is with us," he said to himself. "We're at the national park and Charm is with us. We're at the national park and Charm is with us."

Goliath reckoned if you said something enough times, it came true. He was always saying things like "I can fit another swamp slug into my mouth, I can fit another swamp slug into my mouth," and sometimes he could.

Limpy realized that the noise of the bus engine had stopped too. He could hear another noise now, and it wasn't how he'd imagined a national park would sound.

It was a roar.

A loud roar that wasn't getting softer or coming to an end, just going on and on and on.

What could it be? A huge campground generator? A very angry wild pig? A truck upside down in a ditch with its accelerator jammed on?

It didn't really sound like any of those.

Then another thought came to Limpy.

He'd heard a roar like that before, but not so close.

It was the roar of a plane.

Limpy had seen them often, flying high over the swamp, and a wise old buzzard had told him all about them.

This bus is on the ground, thought Limpy, which means the plane must be on the ground too. Which means we're probably at an airport. Which means there could be lots of planes.

A horrible possibility was growing in his mind.

Panic started to churn in his guts.

What if the humans get onto the planes with their luggage? thought Limpy. The pilots will wind up the big rubber bands and we could all be flown to different places. Me and Goliath and Charm might never see each other again.

"Quick!" yelled Limpy. "Goliath. Charm. We've got to get out of here."

Limpy felt for the hole he'd chewed in the paper bag and ripped it into a bigger hole and scrambled through. He fought his way up through a tangle of human clothes and shoes to what he hoped was the top of the rucksack.

Yes, that felt like a flap. He'd seen them on wombats' bottoms.

Limpy wrestled it open and dragged himself out.

As his eyes slowly got used to the dim light, he saw that the luggage compartment of the bus was huge. Rucksacks were piled almost as far as he could see.

"Goliath," he croaked. "Charm. Where are you?"

"Here," said Goliath's muffled voice.

Limpy threw himself at the rucksack he thought the voice had come from. He got the rucksack open and heaved out human clothes wildly.

There were Goliath's legs.

Limpy grabbed them and hauled on them.

"Hey," protested Goliath as he emerged. "I'm eating. There's a hat in there that's full of white flaky stuff that's really yummy. Like dried coconut, only better."

"We've got to go," said Limpy. "But first we've got to find Charm."

22

Limpy scrambled to all corners of the luggage compartment, yelling Charm's name over and over, hoping desperately that Goliath's repeating trick would work this time.

It did.

"Down here," called a tearful voice.

"Yes," shouted Goliath. "She's here. We've found her." He kissed something in his fist. "Thank you, lucky rabbit poo."

Limpy felt faint with relief.

He dragged Goliath down a mountain of luggage and there was Charm, kissing something herself.

When Limpy saw what she was doing, he felt such a glow of love that he almost forgot the danger they were in.

But not quite.

Gently he pulled her away from the paper bag and

from the lips of the shiny cane toad inside it.

"I was just giving him the kiss of life," said Charm. "To try and revive him. He might not be completely dead."

"Charm," said Limpy softly. "He's full of sawdust."

"So what?" said Charm tearfully. "Goliath eats heaps of sawdust."

Limpy sighed and turned to Goliath.

"You explain," he pleaded.

"Explain what?" said Goliath. "I don't understand anything. I don't even understand why a human would keep delicious food in his hat."

Limpy dragged them both toward an air vent. On the way, he told them about the airport.

They listened to the roar.

And understood.

Together the three of them frantically pounded at the air vent with the miniature cricket bat and the tennis racquet and the golf club.

It was no good. The metal strips wouldn't budge.

Then daylight flooded into the gloom of the luggage compartment. Limpy squinted fearfully into the glare.

The bus driver had opened the compartment door and was pulling luggage out.

Limpy grabbed Goliath and Charm and dragged them into the shadows.

"Shall we all get into the same rucksack?" whispered Charm. "At least that way we'll all be together."

Before Limpy could reply, a figure came crawling into the compartment.

Limpy recognized the figure. It was the young human who hadn't wanted to buy him. The boy started dragging bags from the back of the compartment and pushing them out toward the driver.

"Quick!" whispered Limpy. "Into this rucksack."

They were too late. The boy grabbed the rucksack while Goliath was trying to climb into it. Goliath fell back onto Limpy and Charm. The three of them lay there, dazzled by daylight, while the boy stared at them.

"Wow," said the boy. "Live cane toads."

Limpy, trying not to move a muscle, hoped the boy had said something about dead cane toads and putting them back into the rucksack.

No such luck.

The boy's freckled face broke into a grin, and his eyes widened.

Limpy knew that look. He'd seen human kids give that look to possums and mice and wallabies in campsites. It was the look humans gave to animals they wanted as pets.

"Hop for it," he croaked to Charm and Goliath.

Too late again.

134

The boy picked them up in a wriggling armful and dropped them in a tangled heap down into his windbreaker.

Limpy moved his bottom off Goliath's face and took Charm's elbow out of his mouth. He could feel the boy's hand supporting them on the other side of the windbreaker, which was rocking from side to side as the boy crawled.

Then they all went into a tangle again.

Limpy guessed the boy had climbed out of the bus and stood up. Now it felt as if the boy was walking.

"I'm gunna bite through this cloth," growled Goliath, "and spray him."

Limpy thought about this. It seemed a reasonable thing to do under the circumstances. Then he thought about the boy's friendly freckled face.

"No," said Limpy. "He just wants us to be his pets. Maybe he'll be happy with just one of us. He can have me."

"No," said Charm, gripping Limpy's head.

Limpy gently pulled himself away. "I've got virus germs," he said. "You two might not. It's better you both find the national park and get Mum and Dad and the others there."

"No," said Charm again.

"I'm definitely gunna spray him," said Goliath.

Before Goliath could start chewing the windbreaker,

the boy's hands reached down inside it and lifted the three of them out.

Limpy started to tell Goliath and Charm to look really bad-tempered and unfriendly so the boy wouldn't want them as pets. He stopped when he realized the boy was placing all three of them on the ground.

"Go on," said the boy, smiling. "Hop it before the souvenir hunters get you."

Limpy hoped the boy was saying, "I only want the one with the crook leg; you other two grumpy-looking ones can go." Then he realized the boy was gesturing for all three of them to go.

"Come on," said Charm.

Limpy looked up at the boy, who was still smiling at them. For a fleeting moment he felt he wouldn't mind being a pet with a human like that. If his life had turned out differently.

"Thanks," he said to the boy.

He knew the boy couldn't understand him, but he hoped the boy could see the gratitude in his eyes.

"Come on," said Charm.

The three of them hopped away as fast as they could, Goliath and Charm on either side of Limpy so he wouldn't hop crooked.

Limpy glanced back at the boy, who waved to them and started walking back toward the bus.

136

The roar was louder than ever.

Limpy looked anxiously toward the plane to make sure it wasn't going to take off and squash them.

What he saw stopped him mid-hop.

It wasn't a plane.

It was a huge torrent of water plummeting down a sheer hillside. The humans were leaning over a fence, taking photos of it. The roar was from the water smashing into the rocks below.

"Stack me!" squeaked Goliath.

"A giant waterfall," gasped Charm.

But it wasn't the fresh, cool water that made Limpy's glands tremble and his warts tingle. Even though his parched nose could smell that there wasn't enough salt in it to flavor a single chip.

It was what lay beyond. A green and fragrant landscape that seemed to go on forever. Mighty trees and lush undergrowth and shady swamps buzzing with happy swamp life.

Limpy knew what it was.

He'd never been more sure.

It was toad heaven.

The national park was everything Limpy had dreamed of.

Big.

Beautiful.

Safe.

Very swampy.

Once the three of them were far enough away from the bus, Limpy really started to enjoy it.

"Look," he said, hopping between massive tree trunks. "It's shady here all day. Dad's always worried he'll get headaches from the sun if he leaves our swamp. He won't here."

"And Mum's skin won't dry out," said Charm, gazing around happily. "She's always saying that away from the swamp she'd need huge supplies of caterpillar-intestine skin moisturizer. Not here."

"And the food here's really yummy," said Goliath, slurping a fat slug.

Limpy stopped at the edge of a huge swamp and breathed in the warm moist fragrant air through every pore in his body.

He looked at Charm and Goliath's happy faces.

This is perfect, he thought.

Then he remembered the virus germs that were wriggling around inside him and breathing in the healthy air and getting bigger and stronger by the moment.

Maybe the same with Charm.

Maybe the same with Goliath.

Limpy didn't want to think about that.

"This'll be a great spot for our new place," he said, pointing up at the canopy of leaves over their heads. "Mum's always wanted higher ceilings."

"And she loves this shade of green," said Charm.

"The food here really is great," said Goliath, gobbling a big grasshopper.

Limpy gazed out across the still water. On the opposite bank of the swamp, under a tangle of creepers that looked perfect for climbing up and swinging off, was something that sent a shiver of excitement down Limpy's spine.

"Look at that mud slide," he said. "It's almost as

good as the one at home. This really is heaven. Not only is it a place where all living things are safe and protected, but it's got an almost perfect mud slide."

"Wow," said Charm. "That's the second best mud slide I've ever seen."

"And this," said Goliath, chomping a huge butterfly, "is the best food I've ever tasted."

Afterward, Limpy was never sure why this particular chomp, out of all of Goliath's chomps and gobbles and slurps, was the one that gave him the horrible thought.

But it did.

Limpy stared at Goliath's jaws and felt cold dread seep through his glands and warts.

Charm must have seen the expression on his face, because she grabbed his arm.

"Limpy," she said. "What's the matter?"

Limpy could hardly get it out, but he knew he had to.

"If this national park is a place where all living things are safe and protected, that must mean slugs and grasshoppers and butterflies are safe and protected too. And ants."

He pointed to the ant on the tip of Goliath's tongue.

"Yeah, that's reasonable," said Goliath, swallowing. "What's your point?"

Limpy felt Charm's grip tighten on his arm, and he knew she'd got his point.

His awful, terrible, tragic point.

"My point," said Limpy quietly, "is that if all living things here are protected, what are we going to eat?"

The blood drained from Goliath's warts.

He stared at Limpy, his mouth opening and closing as he tried to think of an answer.

"That's dopey," he said after a bit. "Food can't be protected."

"Yes it can," said Limpy sadly. "All living things means all living things."

"Goliath," said Charm. "Imagine if you were food. You'd want to be protected here, wouldn't you?"

"But I'm not food," said Goliath. "Nothing can eat us. One taste of our poison pus and they've got terminal bellyache."

Limpy looked at Goliath unhappily and waited for the horrible truth to sink in.

Eventually it did.

"This is ridiculous!" shouted Goliath. "If we're not allowed to eat any living thing, how are we going to survive here?"

"Exactly," said Limpy.

"Exactly," said a voice from inside a nearby clump of undergrowth.

They all looked over, startled, as a large lizard emerged.

"Your slightly damaged friend is right," said the lizard to Goliath. "You can't live here."

"He's my cousin," said Goliath hotly. "And he's not damaged, that's a war wound. And if we can't live here, what are you doing here? You blokes are always stuffing yourselves with insects."

Good point, thought Limpy. Goliath can be a real surprise sometimes. His brain must work better when he's angry.

The lizard moistened his lips with his blue tongue.

"Ah," he said. "It's slightly different for me. I'm food, you see. Food is allowed to eat food. All sorts of big creatures have got me on their menu. I eat little things, big things eat me. That's fair. But you eat little things and nothing eats you. That's not fair."

Goliath stared at the lizard, gobsmacked.

"Actually," said Limpy, "we might be food. I've heard rumors of crows out west who've learned to flip us over and eat the soft juicy bits on the insides of our legs and tummies."

Goliath crossed his legs and looked pale.

"Sorry," said Limpy to Goliath and Charm.

"That's okay," said Charm. "I've heard that too."

"Rumors," said the lizard sourly. "I'm talking about

rules, not rumors. The fact is, you're not food, so you can't live here."

Goliath glared at the lizard.

"What if we come back here with millions of our mates?" he asked. "Who's gunna stop us living here then?"

Limpy watched anxiously. He saw Charm was too. When Goliath got worked up, things could get ugly.

The lizard thought calmly about this.

"If there were enough of you, we probably couldn't stop you," he said. "Nor could the national park rangers. But it wouldn't be much of a toad heaven, would it? A place where all the other inhabitants hated you and an army of rangers was trying to kill you."

"Might be," said Goliath hotly.

"No," said Limpy sadly. "It wouldn't."

Goliath turned angrily to Limpy.

"Don't agree with this crawler," he said. "What are you saying?"

"I'm saying," said Limpy, "that if we want to live here, we're going to have to change our diet."

"This mud," said Goliath, "tastes yucky."

Limpy sighed.

Goliath was right.

Even when you made it into mouse and cockroach shapes and added grass stems as whiskers, it still tasted like . . . mud.

"Spit it out, then," said Limpy.

"No," said Goliath indignantly. "I'm not gunna waste it."

He swallowed it with a grimace.

"I don't think this is going to work," said Charm. "I know I haven't got much appetite, but I don't think I'm ever going to be able to swallow these twigs."

She took a wad of wet twigs from her mouth and showed Limpy.

He saw what she meant. She'd been sucking them for ages and they still hadn't gone soft.

Oh dear, thought Limpy. Perhaps this wasn't such a good idea.

"I'm sick of this," said Goliath. "We've been squatting by this dumb swamp all morning trying to change our diet, and it's not working. Those pebbles I swallowed still haven't come out, and they're hurting my tummy."

Limpy nodded sympathetically.

The dead leech he'd eaten hadn't agreed with him either. Every time he burped he could still taste the mold.

"We've got to think harder," said Limpy. "There must be other things we can try that aren't living."

He saw Goliath's tongue dart out.

"Goliath," said Limpy wearily. "Please don't eat ants."

"I need something to take away the taste of the mud," protested Goliath.

Charm hopped to her feet.

"How about the things Goliath was eating in the rucksacks?" she said. "Socks and deodorant sticks and hat flakes. We could try living on human stuff."

"Good thought," said Goliath.

"It is," said Limpy. "But humans aren't allowed to feed animals in national parks, and I just don't think they're going to accidentally drop enough socks to keep us alive."

"I've got it!" yelled Goliath. "I'll break into their buses while they're taking photos of the waterfall and nick stuff. Skin cream, toothpaste, hairbrushes . . ."

Limpy shook his head.

"All right," said Goliath. "I'll scrape dead insects off the fronts of the buses. That's not stealing, that's cleaning."

"Another good thought," said Limpy. "But we came here to get away from humans, not have you risk your neck getting too close to them."

"I don't mind," said Goliath. "Honest."

"I don't either," said Charm.

Limpy looked at them both and his eyes pricked with love for them.

"I know you don't," he said quietly. "I don't either. But we don't want Mum and Dad and the others risking their necks with buses, do we? Because, well, we might not be around for . . . you know . . . forever."

Limpy looked at Charm and Goliath. He could tell from their glum faces that they knew what he meant.

"I haven't got any more ideas," said Charm.

"Nor have I," said Goliath.

"Okay," said Limpy. "There's only one thing left. I'll have to try and persuade the folks here to let Mum and Dad and the others eat live insects."

"How are you going to do that?" asked Charm.

146

Limpy took a deep breath.

"Call a meeting," he said.

The national park residents' committee sat in a row along the top of an important-looking rock.

Limpy sat smiling up at them, trying to look like a good neighbor.

He glanced at Charm, who was sitting next to him, trying to look like a good neighbor too.

He glanced at Goliath, who was sitting on the other side of him with a mouthful of ants.

"Goliath!" hissed Limpy furiously. "Stop it!"

Goliath looked blankly at Limpy; then his face fell.

"Sorry," he whispered. "I forgot."

The blue-tongue lizard took his place at the center of the rock.

"As chairman of the residents' committee," he said, "I declare this meeting open. We're here to consider a residency application from these three cane toads and a horde of others."

"They're not a horde," said Limpy. "They're rellies."

"And they're really kind," said Charm.

"And funny," said Goliath. "Uncle Laurie can blow mucus bubbles that look like frog intestines."

Limpy glared at him.

"Sorry," whispered Goliath.

The committee were muttering too, among

themselves. They turned back to face Limpy and Charm and Goliath.

"I vote no," said the possum.

"I vote no," said the echidna.

"I vote no," said the bat.

"I vote no," said the python.

"I vote no," said the brush turkey.

"I vote no," said the spider.

"I vote no," said the dragonfly.

"And I vote no," said the blue-tongue lizard.

Limpy stared at them, stunned.

"You can't," he croaked. "You haven't heard me speak yet."

"We don't need to," said the lizard. "We've decided."

"Please," said Limpy, "listen to me. I know cane toads have a reputation for being greedy and selfish and eating everything that moves. And it's true, we have been like that. But we can change. And we can be fair. We'll make ourselves available as food. If you let us live here with you, I promise we'll keep our poison sacs empty so we can be eaten too."

Limpy felt Charm frantically digging him in the ribs.

He knew Charm and Goliath wouldn't like hearing this, but he hoped they'd understand when they thought about it.

"None of us wants to die," said Limpy to the committee. "But eating and being eaten is a million times better than being hunted down and squashed under the wheels of a truck. At least being eaten earns the right for other loved ones to eat. Being squashed is just a waste. I know. I've got flat rellies stacked up to my bedroom ceiling."

Limpy paused.

Suddenly the memory of all those poor dead uncles and aunts and cousins was making his eyes fill with tears. Especially the thought of Mum and Dad joining them.

He peered through his mucus at the committee, who had gone all blurry.

Were they listening?

Was that the brush turkey dabbing her eyes?

Limpy's heart skipped a beat.

They are listening, he thought.

Charm was still jabbing him in the ribs.

"Limpy," she hissed.

He ignored her. This was too important.

"Please," he said to the committee, wiping his eyes. "We can change if you just give us a chance."

He looked up and saw that the committee were on their feet and crowding over to one end of the rock.

Limpy didn't understand. Why were they doing this? Was this some sort of voting process?

Then he saw why.

Goliath was standing at the other end of the rock.

He had a dreamy expression on his face and a dragonfly wing poking out of his mouth.

"Goliath!" screamed Limpy. "No!"

Goliath looked toward Limpy, puzzled. Then his face collapsed into anguish.

"Sorry, Limpy," he said. "I forgot again."

The committee, grim-faced, escorted them to the park gate.

"I don't suppose Goliath saying he's sorry for eating a committee member would make any difference," said Charm.

The lizard shook his head.

"It's not fair," said Goliath. "I'm the one you should be keeping out, not all the others. If I promise never to come back, will you let the others in?"

The lizard shook his head.

Limpy steered Charm and Goliath away from the committee.

"Let's go," he said sadly. "I was wrong. This isn't the place for us."

Charm and Goliath stared at him, and Limpy could see they didn't understand why he was giving up.

He pointed up at the gate, to the horrible sight he'd just spotted.

Hanging off the wire mesh were the flat bodies of several cane toads.

Charm gave a sob.

Goliath's shoulders slumped.

"The rangers have got four-wheel drives," said the lizard. "And they're really good at aiming them. Just in case you're thinking of sneaking back in."

"No," said Limpy. "We aren't."

"Mongrels," muttered Goliath.

Limpy led Goliath and Charm away from the gate and away from the park.

He didn't look back.

He didn't want to catch a glimpse of the shady trees or the fragrant swamp or the almost perfect mud slide or the lovely high leafy ceilings that Mum and Dad would have loved so much.

It was too painful now.

Limpy made himself stop thinking about it.

"Come on," he said to Charm and Goliath. "Let's get off this road before a vehicle comes and we end up on the gate."

He led them down a slope to the edge of the river.

They sat on the cool mud.

"What are we going to do now?" asked Charm.

Limpy didn't have a clue.

"I'm sorry," whispered Goliath tearfully. "It's all my fault."

Limpy put his arm round Goliath and struggled to speak over the sick feeling of defeat that was curdling his guts.

"It's not your fault," he said to Goliath. "The national park was my idea, and I got it totally, utterly, completely wrong. It's my fault."

"Thanks," said Goliath.

Charm looked at them both sadly. "It's no one's fault," she said, giving them both a squeeze. "We tried our best."

They sat staring at the wide flat river, which was turning pink in the sunset.

Limpy found himself wondering where Mum and Dad and the others were now, and whether Malcolm had done a better job of finding them a safe place to live.

"I hope Malcolm's had better luck than us," he said. He meant it.

Goliath and Charm nodded thoughtfully.

"His national park might be different," said Goliath.

Limpy stared at him.

"What do you mean?"

"Malcolm's national park might be a bit more welcoming," said Goliath. "To cane toads."

Limpy grabbed Goliath. "Malcolm's national park?" he said. "What do you mean, Malcolm's national park?"

"The national park," said Charm, "that Malcolm is taking Mum and Dad and the others to. The one way out west. What's it called? Um . . ."

"Kickapoo," said Goliath.

"Kakadu," said Charm.

Limpy gaped at them, trying to take this in.

"A national park?" he croaked. "Malcolm?"

"Some galahs from out west told him about it," said Charm. "He wasn't interested at first."

"Then he stole the idea from you," said Goliath. "Typical."

"You knew that," said Charm. "Didn't you?"

Limpy staggered to his feet. "No" just didn't express all the feelings that were bursting out of him.

"If Malcolm was taking you and the others to a national park," he said, "why didn't you stay with him? Why did you go to all this trouble to come to a national park with me?"

"Because we wanted to be with you," said Goliath.

"Because we wanted to look after you," said Charm.

"Plus Mr. Real Estate's plans were making us puke," said Goliath. He glanced at Charm. "Well, some of us."

Limpy looked at their dear concerned faces.

I'm the luckiest cane toad in the whole universe, he thought miserably. Even though I'm also the unluckiest.

"We've got to go back and warn Mum and Dad," he said. "Kakadu could be like the park we've just been to. If they wander in thinking it's toad heaven, they won't stand a chance against the rangers' four-wheel drives. Come on, or we'll be too late."

"They won't be there yet," said Charm. "According to the map Malcolm nicked from the scientist, Kakadu is way out west."

"Good," said Limpy. "That'll give us a chance to catch up with them. Let's go."

Limpy stopped.

A horrible thought had just hit him.

A thought that made him want to weep with despair and squirt poison pus into every human scientist's lunch.

"The virus germs," he croaked. "We can't go back, or we might give them to Mum and Dad and the others."

There was a long silence.

Charm and Goliath looked at each other.

"Limpy," said Charm quietly. "They might . . . they could . . ." She seemed to be having difficulty getting the words out. "Mum and Dad might already have the virus germs."

Limpy slumped at the thought.

"I know," he said. "The scientist's dog said they were going to try and spread them to all cane toads."

"I don't mean that," said Charm. "I mean . . . I mean they might already have caught them from Malcolm."

Limpy staggered and sat down. His legs didn't feel as though they could hold him anymore.

"Malcolm?" he croaked. "How?"

"When Malcolm got back from pinching the map from the scientist," said Charm, "he had a scabby lump on his back a bit like yours."

"Only his was bigger," said Goliath. "And better-looking."

Limpy slowly digested this. The scientist must have injected Malcolm too. So Malcolm could pass the virus germs on to all the others. This was terrible. This was awful. This was the worst news of all.

Mum and Dad with virus germs.

The thought was so painful Limpy couldn't bear it.

He realized dimly that his crook leg and his back

lump were both throbbing. But not as much as his head.

He looked at Charm and Goliath.

"Why didn't you tell me?" he croaked.

Charm and Goliath looked at each other again.

Limpy could see how miserable they were.

"When we saw your back and heard about the virus germs," said Charm, "we weren't totally sure Malcolm's lump was the same."

"We thought it might just have been an infected pimple," said Goliath. "Or an ingrown wart."

Charm gave a big sigh.

"The truth is," she said, "it was too painful and scary to think about. And we didn't want to upset you. There wasn't anything you could have done. Sometimes, Limpy, there isn't anything you can do."

Limpy dragged himself to his feet.

"Yes there is!" he yelled. "It might not be too late. Mum and Dad might not have caught the germs yet. We can go back and find them and keep our distance and stick Goliath's mouth shut with sticky sap and warn them with flying beetles."

Limpy looked around wildly and saw a big log floating sluggishly past on the river.

"Come on!" he shouted. "This river comes from the west. We can paddle ourselves back on it."

He flung himself off the bank and onto the log.

"No!" yelled Goliath.

"Limpy!" yelled Charm. "Don't!"

This is incredible, thought Limpy furiously. They've kept quiet about the danger Mum and Dad are in, and now they don't even want to go and help.

The log gave a lurch.

Limpy struggled to keep his balance.

He was starting to see why Charm and Goliath were so concerned.

Then, with a jolt of fear, he saw exactly why they were.

The log had two big eyes.

26

The eyes were staring straight at Limpy.

The log didn't look at all happy.

Perhaps, thought Limpy hopefully, they're just big knotholes that look like eyes.

The knotholes narrowed and looked even angrier.

Perhaps not, thought Limpy weakly.

The log snorted at him.

Limpy realized the horrible truth. He was standing on a crocodile.

"Jump!" screamed Charm on the riverbank behind him.

"Say you're sorry!" shouted Goliath.

Before Limpy could jump, his legs turned to jelly.

Before he could say anything, his throat sac turned to jelly too.

The crocodile raised its head out of the water. Limpy saw he was on the crocodile's snout. He nearly fainted. He fell forward and clung onto the crocodile's skin bumps with both hands and his good leg, trying not to look at the huge teeth crowding out of the sides of the crocodile's mouth.

"Sorry," he managed to croak. "I thought you were a . . ."

Limpy hesitated. "Log" didn't sound very flattering. Limpy remembered how Ancient Eric used to call Goliath a log in insect math class when Goliath didn't know his bee times-table.

". . . turbo-powered river vessel," croaked Limpy.

The big eyes blinked.

And the mouth started to open.

Limpy fought to control his bladder. He wasn't thinking clearly, but he was pretty sure doing a wee up a crocodile's nose wouldn't be a good idea.

The crocodile's mouth opened more.

Limpy was dimly aware of voices behind him on the riverbank.

"No!" screamed Charm.

"He's got poison pus!" yelled Goliath. "If you eat him, you'll get a bellyache!"

"And he's been injected with germs!" shouted Charm. "That bump on his back is full of them! So he's in no way a health food."

Limpy felt himself moving backward at speed. Then the snout flipped and he somersaulted through

160

the air and landed facedown in the mud of the river-bank.

I don't believe it, thought Limpy, frozen with terror and relief. The croc's thrown me back.

"Thank you," he croaked, too weak to turn round.

He waited for Charm and Goliath to come and help him up.

After a bit, he realized they weren't coming. They were standing well back, clutching each other and screaming things like "Look out!" and "Behind you!" and "Hop for it!"

Limpy looked over his shoulder.

And nearly fainted again.

The crocodile was half out of the water, and its massive wide-open jaws were moving closer, filling the blood-red sky.

"Stop," said Limpy. "You don't have to do this. I know you're not really a vicious coldhearted scavenger. That's just the way humans see you. I know that inside you're warm and kind."

The jaws didn't slow or waver.

They kept coming down until Limpy was swallowed up in their darkness.

The darkness slid from Limpy's eyes.

Limpy realized it wasn't darkness, it was mud.

He sat up.

"Ow."

His back hurt a lot.

Charm and Goliath were bending over him. Charm was doing something to his back.

"Ouch," said Limpy. "Don't."

"I'm trying to stop the bleeding," said Charm.

Limpy didn't understand. He'd just been bitten by a crocodile. By rights, all Charm should be able to do at this point was try and fit him into a hamburger bun.

"Stack me," said Goliath. "This is weird."

Limpy was about to agree when he saw that Goliath was holding a small square of black plastic.

"This was in your back," said Goliath. "The croc bit your lump and it popped out."

Limpy still didn't understand. Why would the croc only bite his back lump when there was a whole back and a head and two arms and one and a half legs to chew on?

"Tracking device," said a deep rumbling voice behind Limpy.

Limpy nearly jumped out of his skin.

He squirmed painfully around.

The crocodile was sprawled half out of the water, massive jaws resting on the bank, looking at the piece of plastic Goliath was holding.

"I knew that lump on your back wasn't virus germs," said the crocodile. "My brother-in-law had

162

one, only bigger and uglier. Tracking device. Human scientists put them in so they can keep track of us. Sends out signals they can pick up miles away."

Limpy stared at the crocodile, then took the square of plastic and stared at it.

"A tracking device?" he said to the crocodile.

The crocodile looked at Charm and Goliath. "Not very quick, is he?"

"He's in shock," said Charm. "We all are."

"So was my brother-in-law," said the crocodile. "Went with his missus on a second honeymoon up north. Next thing he knew a chopper full of humans appeared out of nowhere and took them both off to a farm."

"A farm?" said Limpy nervously. "What sort of farm?"

"A crocodile farm," said the crocodile very slowly, rolling its eyes at Charm and Goliath.

"I knew that," said Goliath.

The crocodile leaned forward and took the tracking device out of Limpy's hand with its front teeth and crunched it into pieces.

"Does this mean," said Charm to the crocodile, her voice wavering, "that Limpy doesn't have virus germs?"

"When did the scientist jab you?" said the crocodile to Limpy. "If that's not too hard a question."

Limpy thought hard. "Four days ago," he said.

"If you had virus germs," said the crocodile, "you'd have been dead two days ago." The crocodile gave a wistful snort. "Number of rabbits I had to spit out a few years ago."

Limpy turned to Charm and Goliath. He could tell from their faces that they had the same joy and relief exploding inside them as he did.

"I haven't got germs!" he yelled.

"You haven't got germs!" they yelled.

"None of us have!" yelled Limpy.

After he'd hugged them both several times, he turned tearfully to the crocodile.

"Thank you," said Limpy. "Thank you."

"That's okay," said the crocodile. "I'm not really a coldhearted scavenger. That's just the way humans see me. Inside, I'm warm and kind."

Limpy flung his arms round the crocodile's jaws and kissed it on the snout.

"Don't push it," said the crocodile.

Limpy turned back to Charm and Goliath for more relieved hugs with them.

A wonderful thought hit him.

"Malcolm hasn't got germs either," said Limpy. "Which means Mum and Dad haven't."

Then Limpy sat down.

Another thought had just paralyzed him quicker than his first sight of the croc's molars.

Malcolm's back bump. The scientist must have put a tracking device in Malcolm too. Which means, thought Limpy miserably, that the humans probably know where Malcolm and Mum and Dad and the others are. They could swoop down on them and wipe them out at any time.

"Oh no," groaned Limpy.

"What's the matter?" asked Charm.

Limpy explained what the matter was. Then he slumped back onto the mud. Suddenly it was all too much. The thought of a chopper coming out of nowhere and doing terrible things to Mum and Dad was more than he could bear, and he didn't even know what a chopper was.

Goliath, groaning, slumped next to him.

"It's hopeless," moaned Goliath. "The humans probably know where we are too."

"It's not hopeless," said Charm. "We were going back to warn Mum and Dad about the germs. We can go back to warn them about this."

Limpy looked up at her determined little face. Just the sight of it made his despair start to fade.

She was right.

Limpy turned to the crocodile.

"Any chance of a lift upriver?" he asked.

"Don't push it," said the crocodile.

Limpy was grateful the train carriage was empty.

This was the first uncrowded part of the whole trip back.

The banana truck from the river to town had not only been bumpy, it had been crowded with spiders, mosquitoes, and snakes. Then, when the three of them had found the station, it had been swarming with humans and sheep.

Now, at last, thought Limpy, here's a chance for us to get some rest.

If only Goliath felt the same.

"Shouldn't we be watching out for everyone?" Goliath was saying, peering out between the planks in the carriage wall, squinting in the morning sun that twinkled through the trees they were clattering past.

Even though Limpy was exhausted, he understood Goliath's concern.

"No need till we get to the railway crossing," said Limpy. "Mum and Dad and the others were heading west, so they'll be somewhere on the other side of that."

Goliath frowned.

Limpy sighed and started to get up out of the comfortable bed he'd made for himself from scraps of soft sheep's wool. He could explain things better standing up.

Charm laid a hand on his arm.

"It's okay," she said. "I'll draw him a diagram."

"There it is!" yelled Goliath. "Our railway crossing!"

Limpy leaped up and peered out.

Goliath was right.

Limpy watched, throat sac tight with emotion, as his old life slid past the carriage.

The railway-crossing light, bare of flying insects in the midday sun.

The highway—unadorned, Limpy was relieved to see, by any squashed rellies.

The tree where Goliath had failed to break Ancient Eric's leaf-bug-eating record, but only because he had a swamp rat in his mouth at the time.

"I could do it now," muttered Goliath, gazing back at the tree. "I know I could."

Limpy strained to catch a last glimpse of his dear home.

Then it was gone.

He looked at Charm and Goliath, and he could see they were thinking the same thing as him.

Will we ever see it again?

From that point on, they didn't take their eyes off the landscape, desperate not to miss anything that looked even a bit like Mum or Dad or Malcolm.

Limpy took one side of the carriage, Goliath the other, and Charm divided her time between the two.

"There!" screamed Goliath, pointing at a paddock. "There's Malcolm!"

"No," said Charm. "It's just a big pile of old horse poo."

She came back over to Limpy.

"Do you really think we'll be able to see them from here?" she said.

Limpy had been wondering the same thing.

"The railway line and the highway both run west," he said. "They'll need to follow one of them, and the railway line's safer. I don't think even Malcolm's crazy enough to go on the highway."

Limpy glanced at Charm.

She didn't reply.

They were so busy peering out, they didn't see the ants come in.

"Hey," said a cross voice. "What're you doing in our carriage?"

Limpy spun round.

A swarm of angry red ants were glaring at him and Charm.

Charm barely took her eyes off the passing country-side. "Your carriage?" she said, glancing over her shoulder. "Who says?"

"We do," said the front ant.

Limpy laid a reassuring hand on Charm's.

He recognized the ants. They were the same sort who'd scared the sheep back at the station.

Stay calm, he said to himself. We don't have time to get into an argument with pushy ants.

"We're hoping to meet up with our rellies," Limpy said to the ant. "Out west."

"Same here," said the ant. "So rack off."

On the other side of the carriage, Goliath was looking at the ants and licking his lips.

Limpy held up his hand, signaling to Goliath to stay where he was.

"I'm going to need your help," said Limpy to the ants. "I'm trying to encourage my cousin over there not to eat every ant he sees, and he's trying hard, but I'm afraid he's finding you almost impossible to resist."

The ants looked at Goliath and saw the hunger in his eyes.

Limpy saw their expression change as they realized they were looking at a toad who'd eat every single one of them, even if he had to find a needle and sew a gusset in his tummy.

The ants looked at one another.

"Our mistake," scowled the front ant. "Our carriage must be the next one."

They scurried away.

"Hey," said Goliath, disappointed. "Why did you do that?"

"I'm trying to get us in the habit," said Limpy, "of being kinder to insects when we're not hungry."

"But I *am* hungry," said Goliath.

Much later they still hadn't seen any sign of Mum or Dad or Malcolm or anyone.

Limpy had the idea of climbing up through the air vent onto the roof of the carriage for a better view. Even though the train was on a slow stretch, it wasn't an easy climb. Goliath got jammed in the vent, and Limpy and Charm had to use all their mucus to slide him through.

After all that, being on the roof didn't make any difference.

Still not a rellie to be seen.

This isn't looking good, thought Limpy, the warm afternoon breeze doing nothing to relieve the worried ache in his glands.

Could we have missed them? he wondered. Or could they have taken another route? Or could they already be at Kakadu, hanging from the front gate?

There were so many possibilities, and Limpy didn't like the thought of any of them.

"I haven't seen a single cane toad," said Charm, sounding as worried as Limpy felt.

"Me neither," said Goliath from the other side of the carriage roof. "All I can see are donkeys and goats and foxes and brumbies and camels and feral pigs."

Limpy slithered quickly across the roof to Goliath in case the sun was affecting his cousin's brain and Goliath decided he could fly or something.

When Limpy got there, his mouth fell open.

Not far from the train was an incredible sight.

A huge crowd of animals, hundreds of them, including all the ones Goliath had mentioned, moving slowly across the dusty scrubland.

Why are they going so slowly? wondered Limpy.

Then he saw why.

Leading them was a group of much smaller figures, hopping wearily. The one in front was less small and was studying a map.

"Look!" yelled Charm, arriving next to Limpy. "That's Malcolm!"

"And there's Dad!" screamed Limpy.

"Stack me," muttered Goliath. "I thought they were rocks."

Limpy squinted down at the dusty cane toads. Where was Mum? He couldn't see Mum.

"Mum!" he yelled. "Mum!"

"They can't hear us," said Charm.

"Come on!" yelled Limpy to Charm and Goliath. "Time to get off. Jump! Jump!"

"Limpy!" yelled Mum.

Limpy, even though he was still dizzy from being whacked in the head by the ground, could see that Mum's eyes were wide with delight.

His were too as he zigzagged over and flung his arms round her and Dad.

Limpy lost track of time in a chaos of hugs and tears and backslaps and questions and a mild concussion.

He even found himself hugging Goliath at one stage and asking him how things had been going.

"Not bad," said Goliath. "Though when I jumped off the train I swallowed my tongue, and I think part of it's still down my throat."

After Limpy calmed down a bit, he realized how tired and dusty all the cane toads looked.

"Mum," said Charm, concerned. "Look at you. It's too dry out here in the west for you."

"I'll be fine," said Mum, licking her parched lips. "Once we get to Kakadu."

Then Limpy saw Malcolm standing to one side, watching them.

"So," said Malcolm. "You've decided to join me." He pointed dramatically to the hundreds of animals standing patiently in the dust. "As you can see, my real estate investment proposal has become very popular."

Limpy heard uncertain muttering from some of the animals.

"It's not really the investment we're interested in," said a rabbit. "It's the national park."

"A place where all living things can be safe and protected forever," said a donkey.

"And that's exactly what you'll get," said Malcolm. "As soon as you pay up."

Limpy looked at the travel-weary animals. At the yearning expression in their eyes as they peered anxiously toward the western horizon.

I've got to tell them the truth, thought Limpy.

"I'm afraid," he said, "that's probably not what you'll get."

The animals stared at him.

"Me and my sister and cousin have just been to a national park over to the east," said Limpy.

"Two, if you count the permanently flooded one," said Goliath.

"We thought the same as you about national parks," Limpy continued, looking sadly at the animals. "But I'm afraid it's not true. Not all living things are safe and protected there. Only the lucky few that are allowed in."

The animals broke into angry murmuring.

"Bull," said a camel. "You've got that wrong."

"That'd be discrimination," said a fox.

"That's against the law these days," said a mouse.

"Excuse me, everyone," said Goliath to the animals. "This will be important for your application. Do you all get eaten?"

"No," said a wild horse. "Just shot from helicopters."

Limpy looked at Charm for help, but she was frowning anxiously. She pointed to Limpy's back, and then to Malcolm.

Limpy nodded. She was right. They had to destroy Malcolm's tracking device before the humans arrived with guns and golf clubs and big needles.

A feral pig interrupted while Limpy was still working out how to do this.

"That national park to the east," said the pig. "How far away is it?"

"By foot," said Limpy, "a few days. But please, listen to me. . . ."

Limpy was drowned out by a very loud snort from the feral pig, who pointed angrily down to Malcolm.

"That's how far that mongrel reckoned Kakadu was," said the pig. "I reckon it's more like a few months. We'd be better off going east."

The other animals muttered in agreement.

"That's right, you would," said Goliath. "No, hang on, no you wouldn't."

"That's enough!" roared Malcolm.

For a moment Limpy thought Malcolm was going to try and bully the whole crowd of animals, but then he realized Malcolm was yelling just at him.

"How dare you!" thundered Malcolm, towering over Limpy. "I should have flattened you ages ago, and I think I'll do it now."

Limpy took a step back.

Somebody leaped in front of him.

It was Charm, eyes flashing as she glared up at Malcolm.

"Listen, handsome," she said in an icy voice. "You may have a clever business brain and be hunkier than any toad around, but if you touch my brother I'll take you apart wart by wart and feed you to that goat."

"Eh?" said the goat.

Malcolm took a step back. Then he recovered and thrust his head at Limpy.

"How dare you push in here and try to undermine

my business plan," he growled. "What gives you the right?"

"Well," said Limpy. "It's really just the fact that you've been leading my whole family into mortal danger."

"Danger!" said Mum. "What danger?"

"Rubbish!" thundered Malcolm. "My easy-purchase plan offers safety, not danger."

Limpy looked up at the feral pig.

"Excuse me, Mr. Pig," he said. "See that lump on Malcolm's back? Would you mind stabbing it with your tusk?"

"My pleasure," said the pig.

"Hey, wait a minute," protested Malcolm. But before he could move, the pig prodded his back lump with the tip of a tusk.

"Ow!" yelled Malcolm.

The pig withdrew the tusk.

Malcolm stood frozen with shock and pain while a small square of black plastic popped out of his back and landed on the ground.

The animals and cane toads all crowded round and stared at it.

"What's that?" said Dad.

"Did Malcolm swallow a brake pad?" asked Mum.

Limpy explained about the tracking device, Goliath assisting with some of the more technical terms, like "brother-in-law" and "second honeymoon."

"This is ridiculous," snapped Malcolm. "Anyone who thinks that thing can tell humans where we are is an idiot."

"Look," said Goliath, pointing across the scrub. "I think it's telling those humans where we are."

Limpy peered in the direction of Goliath's arm.

And saw a four-wheel drive speeding toward them along a narrow dirt road.

The animals saw it too, and reared up in panic.

"Let's get out of here," said a camel.

"Dead right," said a mouse.

"I'm off to that other national park," said the pig. "Which way's east?"

"This way," said a fox. "Let's go."

Limpy stood dazed as the ground shook and the animals thundered away.

He waited for the four-wheel drive to veer off the road and start rounding the animals up.

But it didn't.

Even when Goliath jumped on the tracking device and cracked it in half, the four-wheel drive continued to speed directly toward Limpy and the other stunned and exhausted cane toads.

178

29

"No!" screamed Malcolm at the four-wheel drive. "Stay away from me! I haven't got that thing in me anymore. Look."

He pushed Limpy out of the way and turned and showed the hole in his back to the rapidly approaching vehicle.

The four-wheel drive didn't even slow down.

"Please," sobbed Malcolm. "Have mercy. I'll never promote a real estate subdivision with unreasonably high interest rates ever again."

The other cane toads were panicking too, and hopping in all directions.

Limpy scrambled to his feet and tried to help Charm and Goliath drag Mum and Dad out of the path of the four-wheel drive. But they got tangled up with Malcolm, who was trying to hide behind them, and they all fell in a heap.

Stack me, thought Limpy. We're not going to make it.

The wheels were heading straight for them.

"Mummy," whimpered Malcolm.

Limpy reached out to hold as many of his family as he could, and wished for their sakes that the world was a fairer place, and waited for the end.

It didn't come.

The four-wheel drive zoomed straight past them.

Limpy looked up through the dust, his heart beating a wobbly rhythm of relief in his ears.

He was feeling a bit confused.

He watched the four-wheel drive screech to a stop next to a low mound of dry earth. Two human blokes with khaki shorts and shirts and no beards got out, flung open the back doors of the vehicle, and dragged out what looked to Limpy like some sort of big squirter attached to a big plastic drum of something.

They started spraying liquid onto the mound.

"What are they doing?" said Goliath in Limpy's ear.

"I think it's an ants' nest," said Limpy.

He felt Charm move closer to him.

"Do they realize they've parked on top of another one?" she whispered.

Limpy swung his gaze back to the four-wheel drive.

She was right. He could see another, smaller mound half covered with dry grass under the vehicle.

Red ants were starting to pour out of it and swarm all over the four-wheel drive.

"Stack me," said Goliath. "It's more of those rude mongrels."

"Fire ants," said Charm. "I overheard some sheep talking about them back at the railway station. They've only been in these parts a short while, and already humans hate them even more than cane toads."

"Really?" said Limpy.

"I don't hate them," said Goliath. "I think they're yummy."

"Don't even think about it," said Charm. "Come on, let's get Mum and Dad under cover."

Before Limpy could move, the humans turned and saw the ants all over their vehicle. They rushed over, beating at them with their hats.

"Why don't they spray it?" said Charm.

"Probably dissolve their duco," said Limpy.

Although he knew he should be helping Mum and Dad, Limpy couldn't tear his eyes away from the humans.

One of the humans had ants swarming up both legs. The human realized, but too late. One of the ants bit him. He flinched from the sting. For all the other ants on his legs, this was a signal. They all bit him together.

The human screamed and fell to the ground, flailing at his legs with his hands.

Stack me, thought Limpy.

Even though humans could be pretty cruel, he didn't like seeing anyone suffer like that.

"Poor mongrel," muttered Goliath. "I know I should be pleased, but I'm not."

Limpy's mind was a whirl of thoughts.

The other human was beating at his mate with a shirt, trying to knock the ants off him. He didn't have a hope. And if the ants bit the first human again, things wouldn't look good.

Limpy turned to Goliath.

"Go on," said Limpy. "Dinnertime."

Goliath's eyes widened with delight.

"Thanks," he said.

He hopped over toward the two humans.

Limpy held his breath and watched. He glanced at Charm. She was watching intently too. Limpy could tell from her expression that she was hoping for the same thing as him.

The human on the ground saw Goliath hopping toward him, and his face twisted with revulsion.

"Arghhh!" he screamed. "Now I'm being attacked by a cane toad! Get away, you ugly brute!"

The other human grabbed a spade from the side of

the four-wheel drive and raised it above his head.

"Goliath!" yelled Limpy. "Look out! Hop for it!"

Goliath didn't hear, or pretended he didn't.

The human with the spade suddenly saw that it was covered in ants and that they were running up his arms. He dropped the spade and started flapping his arms frantically.

The human on the ground was getting pretty frantic too.

Goliath had almost reached his legs.

"Don't bite me!" screamed the human, rolling over and trying to kick Goliath.

Goliath dodged the kick and opened his mouth.

The human screamed again.

Goliath's tongue shot out and slid along the human's leg. In an instant it was coated with ants. Goliath swallowed happily.

The human started to yell some more, then realized what Goliath had done. And, Limpy saw excitedly, was doing again. And again.

The human's face collapsed into relief and amazement as he stared at Goliath's busy tongue. Soon Goliath had eaten all the ants off one leg and was starting on the other.

"You little beauty," gasped the human.

Limpy didn't know what the human had said, but

he could tell the human was pleased. It looked like Goliath could tell too, because he was eating even faster.

The human looked as though he wanted to kiss Goliath.

"Hey, look at this!" he called delightedly to his mate.

"Me next!" yelled the other human, still flapping his arms. "Me next!"

Limpy stood in the mouth of Ancient Eric's cave and surveyed his swamp.

It was looking good.

Everyone was safely home, the snakes were back in the stew, Ancient Eric was out of his pizza box and laid to rest in a properly constructed memorial bog, and the moonlight was gleaming on the water in a way that made Limpy's warts feel more tingly than human soft drink.

I never liked that national park swamp as much as this one, thought Limpy happily. No way.

Mum and Dad hopped over.

"Oh, Limpy," said Mum, her face glowing. "We're so happy to be home."

"We're proud of you, son," said Dad. "When you were a tadpole and that flood washed away most of your brothers and sisters and you got wedged in that rock, I knew you were destined for great things."

"Thanks, Dad," said Limpy, glowing.

Mum gave him a kiss on the warts.

"We're so lucky," she said. "Having you to keep us safe. We're the luckiest cane toads in the whole wide swamp."

Limpy's throat sac trembled with love.

"And that idea of yours was brilliant," said Dad. "Suggesting Charm for leader. She's perfect. She's hardly ever hungry, so she can keep a clear head and make decisions based on wisdom rather than on where the next snake's coming from. No disrespect to Ancient Eric."

Limpy smiled. "I think she's going to be a fine leader," he said.

He felt a tap on the shoulder and turned round.

It was Charm, grinning at him.

"It's a very posh cave," she said. "But I still prefer my room at home."

"Up to you," said Limpy. "You're in charge."

Charm's face fell. "I'm still not sure about this, Limpy. I'm still not sure if I'm ready."

Limpy gave her a gentle squeeze.

"Look," he said. "Over there. I think those kids need some supervision."

A commotion was approaching. A group of little cane toads were rolling a large round object through the undergrowth. The large round object was protesting loudly.

"Ow. Not so fast. They're biting me. Ow. Slow down. Look out, we're heading for a tree. Ouch."

Charm hurried over. Limpy and Mum and Dad followed.

"Girls and boys," said Charm sternly. "I think you might be forgetting some of the things you've been taught about gathering ants." Her voice softened. "Malcolm doesn't like it when you roll him into trees."

Malcolm, covered in sticky sap and red ants, looked balefully up at her.

"Malcolm doesn't like it, full stop," he muttered.

"I'm sorry," said Charm, her voice suddenly steely. "What was that?"

"Nothing," mumbled Malcolm. "Come on, kids, I think I saw another ants' nest over there."

Mum shook her head fondly. "He's a nice young man, that Malcolm," she said. "Well, he is now, since he gave away that real estate nonsense and started helping out around here." She nudged Limpy. "Do you know, I think Charm's keen on him."

Limpy smiled. "Could be," he said.

"And these fire ants are wonderful," said Mum. "Bit spicy at first, but when you get used to them, so versatile in the kitchen."

Limpy smiled again. "We'll have to get you on telly," he said. "I know a few million humans who'd love to hear you say that."

Dad gave a chuckle. "I'll never forget that human fella's face when he saw Goliath eating those ants off his legs. That's the first time I ever saw a human look at a cane toad with respect."

"Well," said Limpy, "I don't think it'll be the last."

He showed Mum and Dad the surprise he'd been saving for them. A page from a newspaper that had been chucked from a car only yesterday.

"Look at the photo," said Limpy.

Filling half the page was one of the photos the two humans had taken after Goliath had finished eating the ants off them. A close-up of a happy Goliath, mouth bulging as he licked ants off the four-wheel drive.

Limpy couldn't read what the headline said, but he was pretty sure it was something like CANE TOAD HERO.

"Doesn't Goliath photograph well?" said Mum.

"And he's got a mighty appetite, that lad," said Dad. "Let's hope he never loses it."

Limpy grinned. "I don't think he will."

Limpy found Goliath in his favorite spot in the swamp, lying in the mud under a fragrant stinkweed bush.

"G'night, Goliath," said Limpy. "You're awake early."

"No time for sleeping in," grinned Goliath. "Too much eating to do."

A little cane toad appeared, carrying a leaf piled with fire ants.

"On top of the empties, thanks," said Goliath.

The little cane toad placed it on a tall stack of empty leaves.

"Shall I bring more, Mr. Goliath?" he asked.

Goliath groaned in pleasant pain. "I'm pretty full," he said. "I can probably only manage another six lots."

"Okay, Mr. Goliath."

Limpy saw that the little cane toad was hovering, trying to pluck up the courage to ask Goliath something.

"Go on," whispered Limpy. "He won't eat you."

"Don't count on that," said an ant.

"Mr. Goliath," said the little cane toad. "Is it true that if you eat fifty lots of fire ants a night, humans won't want to kill us?"

"Something like that," said Goliath. "It might be sixty."

He winked at Limpy.

The little cane toad ran off happily.

Limpy showed Goliath the newspaper photo.

"Thanks, Goliath," said Limpy. "I'm really glad you're my cousin."

Goliath glowed.

"It's a funny thing, Limpy," he said. "We went all that way looking for toad heaven, but if a crow from out west suddenly appeared and flipped me over and ate the soft juicy bits on the inside of my legs and tummy, I wouldn't want it to happen anywhere else but here."

Limpy nodded and smiled.

He knew exactly what Goliath meant.

GLOSSARY

BRUMBY: A wild or untamed horse. Strangely, there is no similar word for a wild or untamed yabbie. (See *yabbie.*)

CARKED: Dead. Always followed by the word "it." As in "Will Wally be coming to Dave's funeral?" "No, he's carked it too."

CHIPS: Small pieces of fried potato. Known in some places as French fries. But not in France, where they are called fried potato.

CROOK: Ill or damaged rather than criminal. Limpy's crook leg is the result of a truck driving over it. At no stage has his crook leg ever tried to rob a bank or falsify corporate accounts.

FLOATIE: An inflatable or foam device to help unsure swimmers stay afloat in pools and at the beach. Can be used in the bath if you're very nervous.

FULL STOP: The little dot at the end of a sentence. Also an expression meaning "not at all." So an Australian would say, "I don't like having to put full stops at the end of sentences, in fact I don't like full stops full stop."

GOBSMACKED: Stunned with surprise and/or amazement. If you ever find yourself gobsmacked while swimming in deep water, perhaps because you see somebody with a floatie shaped like a yabbie, be careful or you could end up carking it. (See *carked, floatie,* and *yabbie.*)

KNICKKNACK: Small ornament beloved by most mothers on their birthdays, but only when purchased legally. (See *nick.*)

MATE: Friend, comrade, buddy. Used a lot when people are being helpful and friendly. "Hey, mate, if that's your wombat over there lying on his back with his legs in the air, I think he's a bit crook." "Thanks, mate." (See *crook.*)

NICK: Two meanings in Australia: (1) Steal. (2) Leave a place briefly. On the occasion of his mother's birthday, a thief might say "I'm just gunna nick out and nick a knickknack." (See *knickknack*.)

WOMBAT: A wild, but mild, Australian animal about the size of an overweight cat. Despite its plumpness, a vegetarian. Lives in a burrow too small for a home gym.

YABBIE: A freshwater crayfish. Can be lured with a piece of meat on a string. This is not recommended if the yabbie is on someone else's plate in a restaurant.

Morris Gleitzman grew up in England and moved to Australia when he was sixteen. He has been a frozen-chicken thawer, sugar-mill rolling-stock unhooker, fashion-industry trainee, department-store Santa, TV producer, newspaper columnist, and screenwriter. Now he's a children's book author. *Toad Heaven* is his fifteenth book.